Brendan Connell

THE HEEL

Brendan Connell was born in Santa Fe, New Mexico, in 1970. His works of fiction include *Unpleasant Tales* (Eibonvale Press, 2013), *The Architect* (PS Publishing, 2012), *Lives of Notorious Cooks* (Chômu Press, 2012), *Miss Homicide Plays the Flute* (Eibonvale Press, 2013), *Jottings from a Far Away Place* (Snuggly Books, 2015), and *Cannibals of West Papua* (Zagava, 2015).

BRENDAN CONNELL

THE HEEL

THE HEEL

One

Climbing the steps up to the second floor I opened and closed my eyes trying to force them awake and then put my hand on the doorknob and turned the handle.

"Good morning," he said.

I agreed that it was a good morning though I really didn't think it was.

It felt like I had spent the night in a Kenmore electric dryer. I had a headache and was dehydrated, and a drink might have made it better, or should I say tolerable, but the bottle had been empty and my wallet was still empty—a few kachina dolls staring at me, cut my throat with a genuine Neolithic bird point, good morning misery if you want to keep taking me on entrapped in that subterranean just he had me in chains one step and I would go miles that thirst that just wouldn't stop can't do it for ever use your thumb stones, blood squirting everywhere okay but I slithered along into my hole every day behind the anthill but then decided to try one of their holes thinking maybe it was some kind of shortcut, feet wallowing in Ming-green slime. Yeah, I probably should have apologized for being late, but I didn't. To hell with it. I was being paid on a wage/per sale basis, and the pickings were small enough to warrant a little tardiness. The funny thing is, the less money you make, the more is expected of you.

George was at his desk, typing up a letter on an old Underwood typewriter and I went into the head and took a leak.

As I was rinsing my hands my eyes shifted up and took note of a cleft chin on a voluminous jaw dotted with stubble and a black helmet of hair ranged above it and a moustache that looked like the wings of a blackbird flying above my upper lip and I wondered how I could look so good and feel so bad. I splashed some water on my face, then wiped it with a paper towel. Bending over, I took a long slurping drink from the tap.

Back in the office, I asked George if there were any orders to fulfill.

"There *were*," he replied curtly. "Twelve orders for arrowheads and one for an engraved brass tomahawk. I posted them twenty minutes ago."

"That's it?"

"That's it. It's your job to drum up the local business."

I took the hint, sat down at my desk and lit a Benson & Hedges. I called the Trading Post down on West Manhattan and asked if they were short on stock. They were not. When I called the Relic Shack, the joker there tried to sell me a load of blankets he had got from Mexico and I laughed half-heartedly and hung up. The truth is that the demand for our products was limited.

The job was simple enough. We sold Indian artifacts, some genuine, some less than. The bulk of our business, if the word bulk could actually be used, was in the mail order arrowhead line. George put ads in *Popular Mechanics* and *Boys' Life* and a few other magazines and we usually got about ninety or a hundred orders for arrowheads a week through the mail. When we sent out the arrowheads we included a crummy catalogue of other more high-end items, and we'd get maybe nine or ten catalogue orders a week.

The rest of the sales were mostly to in-state shops. These were my responsibility. The shops always got product for a fifty percent break in price and I got a ten percent commission on sales. But that meant that I had to unload a thousand arrowheads in a month to get a fifteen dollar commission, which got added to what were probably some of the lowest wages in the country. So I used the arrowheads and other lower ticket items as bait and would try to shove in a few more expensive items while I was at it, and then skim wherever I could.

Truth be told, it probably wasn't the right job for someone of my caliber, but it had to do until something better came along.

At eleven-forty George got up from his chair and said he was going out to get a hamburger sandwich and asked if I wanted one. I told him I was just plain broke, so he said he'd spot me.

"Extra onions on mine," I said.

"To drink?"

I wanted a cerveza but didn't dare ask.

"A Mr. Pibb," I said.

Every now and again, maybe five or six times a week, some chump would walk in and want to buy from us direct, and if I was lucky enough to be able to make those sales, I'd get a commission on that.

About four minutes after George had left, a guy came wandering in who had seen our ad in *The Thrifty Nickel*. He was short and wore glasses and though he probably wasn't much over thirty was already losing his hair. He was from California and was in town for a few days on some sort of business that he didn't elaborate on.

"I wanted to bring something back to my boy who's nine and I thought maybe you'd be cheaper than the guys on the main drag."

"We are," I said. "Most of them buy their stuff from us. So if you get something from us it'll be about half the price of anyone else. And we have a bigger selection. The biggest selection in the state. We have over fifteen thousand items."

He looked around at the limited goods hanging from the walls and sitting on the dusty shelves and blinked.

"They aren't all out, of course," I said. "We have a stockroom in the back, but that's off-limits to clients."

"What's that thing with the feathers over there?"

"That's a genuine Indian war bonnet."

He went over and started looking at it and feeling the feathers and then went and grabbed a sweat lodge drum and tapped on it with his finger making a dull *tock tock tock* sound.

"Buffalo rawhide," I said. "Won't go flat in steam."

He looked around a little bit more, touching just about everything we had out, me pitching the goods, until he finally ended up with the war bonnet in one hand and a pair of beaded elk leather moccasins in the other, child-size, not sure which to get. But I knew I could get more for the war bonnet than the moccasins, so I revved up the old hardsell on the former, deciding that it was probably a pretty *rare* item.

"That one's a beauty," I told him. "A lady from the Native American Museum was here looking at it. I guess they're thinking of purchasing it for their collection."

"You don't say?"

"Well, a genuine Indian war bonnet like that in such prime condition—there are probably not twenty in the country like it."

"I guess I'd be stupid not to get this one."

"Well, I don't know where else you're going to find a museum-grade piece for twenty bucks."

"Gee, twenty dollars seems like a lot."

"Last year one like this sold at auction for ninety-five. Sure, twenty dollars isn't chicken feed, but if you want to do something nice for—what's your kid's name?"

"Joey."

"If you want to do something nice for Joey, purchasing such an article as this might be just the thing."

"Maybe so."

"Joey would probably like some arrowheads too," I told him.

"How much for an arrowhead?"

"They're ten for three dollars."

"I don't know if I need a whole ten."

"Well, giving a kid one arrowhead isn't much of a gift."

"Yeah, I guess you might be right."

"I am right. Arrowheads are like marbles. Can you imagine Joey going to school with one marble and showing it to his friends? But send him off with a bag full of arrowheads and just watch how popular that boy gets."

He ended up buying the war bonnet and ten arrowheads for twenty-three dollars to which I added four percent sales tax bringing it to a total of twenty-three dollars and ninety-two cents. He handed me twenty-five dollars and I took one dollar and eight cents from the cash box and gave that to him as change. Once he had gone, I slipped the twenty-five dollars into my wallet, making a mental note that I owed the cash box one dollar and eight cents, then got another war bonnet from the stock room and put it where the other had been. George had enough arrowheads and Indian paraphernalia that I doubted he'd miss the things—and I figured I needed the twenty-three ninety-two a hell of a lot more than he did.

"Any action?" George asked when he got back.

"Nope."

"Didn't figure."

After eating my hamburger sandwich I started in on the dialing again and must have rung up half the places in the Southwest before I finally got an order from Christine's Curiosity Shop up in Taos, who asked for a half dozen buffalo powder horns and a box of bannerstones.

Right after I hung up, the phone rang. I picked it up, hoping it was a call back with some more business, but it was Yvonne asking me if I wanted to come over for dinner. I didn't really, but hadn't had any high performance since Saturday night, so said I would.

I had a '68 Buick Skylark four-door hardtop that I had bought for $1,540 two years earlier.

After work I ran it over to El Toro and picked up a six-pack of Fischer's Old German Style Ale, a quart of Yellowstone and a deck of Benson & Hedges, then nosed my way over to Yvonne's. It wasn't that I actually wanted to spend time with her so much as I felt I had to see *someone*. I was, after all, a man, and she was, well, a *woman*. And not a bad looking one at that. Hell, most men would have jumped on her like a bear on honey, but for me she just didn't work. It happens like that sometimes. You can't always explain attraction. If I really thought about it, some of the best pleasure I had ever had had been with ugly women.

So, yeah, you really can't explain attraction.

She worked as a cashier at a furniture clearance center, working five days a week, from 9 a.m. to 6 p.m. I had met her four months earlier when I had been doing door to door work for Sweet Dart Cosmetics. She had just been coming off a relationship with a guy who ended up in the can for breaking into pay phones with a crowbar and she had needed some cheering up and cheer her up I did.

"I don't want to go through anything like that again," she told me. "I need someone I can love."

Maybe the problem with Yvonne was that she had *too much* need to love. She liked me too much. Maybe she was just too easy, some tavern girl I could put under my arm and carry wherever I wanted and do whatever I wanted to.

"Serve me spiced oat gruel," I'd say.

"I'll serve you *anything!*"

She lived on a dead-end dirt lane, in an old, unglamorous part of town. Her uncle had left her the place, and she had prettied it up, using her employee discount from where she worked to get nice furniture in there and finding some oil paintings of flowers and deer to put on the walls.

I pulled up to her place and got out with the six-pack in one hand, but left the Yellowstone in the car. She usually had a bottle of something or other around for me, and I'd save mine for later.

I knocked and she opened the door and crushed her lips against mine.

"Oh, honey," she said. "Thank God you came. I was going crazy without you. I thought you were going to come by over the weekend, but you never did."

"Yeah, I had to run down to El Paso to pick up a load of arrowheads and husks," I lied. "George might not pay me much, but he sure does work me hard."

"Lucky him," she said.

I could feel her breath, warm and moist on my face, and almost wished I felt for her like she did for me. But I didn't. I pushed her away.

She was wearing some sort of loose pants and a matching top that were probably fashionable but that didn't do much for her lines. I guess she had no idea that the white pumps she was wearing made her feet look big. She had long, straight black hair and medium-sized breasts and her body had a nice shape to it.

"Did you have a good day?" she asked.

I told her that I hadn't.

"Well, we better make it a good night then. I'm going to cook you something nice."

I drank three beers while she fixed dinner and then we ate a big meal. She had cooked beef enchiladas and prepared a green salad.

The food was good and I ate as much as I could and then I went in the living room and poured myself a half a glass of Hiram Walker's Ten High straight bourbon whisky that she had set out for me and flipped on the TV while she did the dishes. Then she came in and we started watching a show and she began to cuddle up to me, putting her head near mine and pecking at me and feeling around until finally I started to give back as much as she gave.

"Oh, Mitch," she said.

We traded spit for a while and then went to the bedroom and undressed. As her hands pulled me towards her, I forgot that I didn't like her. I pressed my lips to her wet mouth and she started clawing at me like a rangy cat and things began to grow bigger and better. It was quick and frantic and then slow and easy and then quick again. Then I lay there wanting to get the hell out.

"I love you," she said.

I squeezed her shoulder a little, hoping that would do for an answer. She pushed her body up against mine and put her head on my chest. With my left hand I managed to reach over to the nightstand and grab one of her butts and light it. It was a Virginia Slim and tasted like crap, but at least it gave me something to do.

As I lay there, I kept thinking that I would have to get rid of her. It was too much damned work. I didn't mind the meals and balling so much, but the lovey-dovey stuff made me feel like vomiting. By the way she acted I could tell that she thought we had something serious going, but I was about as serious as a Ringling Brothers clown on laughing gas.

I could have kept her awake if I had wanted to, but I didn't and finally she fell asleep. I edged out from under her and snuck out of bed, got dressed and went home.

There was still the bottle of Yellowstone, and that was all the company I needed.

Two

The plane stretched out vastly, the sky and I had wolf hides but kept covered by a sheet of monotonous grey. A few leafless trees stood, vultures and ravens had much of a voice some sort of bard perched in their dire branches. The bleached bones of elephants and men lay here and there, remnants of some battle of times gone by, when the world was young, being hewn into shape by axes and long swords and men displayed their unmitigated lust with scimitars the wettest thing I had ever touched and spears which fell like mellow breast-side kisses and it too was probably wanted like that.

I took charge of my tired mule and was also in possession of a tiredness, but an eagerness as well. I had slept too long on hard things to pay me on the asphalt and sidewalks unemployment lines selling my blood twice a day and empty swimming pools and if I hadn't now wished for a soft bed of feathers and a voluptuous body with which a respectable citizen to unwind my bold passion like bargain basement bourbon spilling all over her.

My mule had a back heavy with hides, which I was bringing to the city of Oghris for trade. I had gathered them together over many moons, hunting in the Sverig Mountains, denied of both woman-flesh and wine and forced to find my pleasure with stout pines and random rocks—to give them my love with only my imaginings to fashion them into the supple limbs of nymphs and wenches who had been eating cantharides rubbing up against everything in sight.

My feet had walked so many leagues, and my bow, which sat unstrung but sensual atop the hides, had discharged so many shafts.

"Come you lazy beast," I said, "we must make the city walls before dark or have desperados to contend with."

The animal looked at me sadly and brayed, knowing perchance that desperados came in the day as well as the night. And, indeed, not many moments after I had uttered my words, three beings sprang up from behind a scattering of large rocks that lay by the way. They had scraggly beards and sun-baked bodies and each carried a sword screwing everything that moved ferocious bandits they were, outcasts hungry to rape the labor of another and with swaying shoulders and wide strides they advanced together and started kissing.

"You, man!" one of them cried out. "Forfeit that donkey full of hides, lest we must send thy soul to wretched Hades!"

I drew out my sword and flexed my broad chest.

"Take ye hence, knaves," I growled. "For if ye want these hides, ye must take my own first."

One, the tallest and leanest of the three, who had on shaggy boots, came charging at me, brandishing vicious his hard blade.

"I shall now sweeten the sand with your blood!" the fellow cried, swinging wildly.

I, Mulvizeg, hunter by birth and trade, lithe as a cat or oiled whip, easily avoided the onslaught and thrust my own blade into this man's groin, and he collapsed with a cry of aguish leaping from his throat, just as the second joined in the fray, attempting to stab me in my heart.

I stepped to the side, hearing his weapon whiz by me, then lifted high my sword and smote him on the crown, cleaving him in two.

"You have killed me!" the other said as he fell to the ground.

The last stood bewildered and frightened.

"Bestow some mercy on me, good sir," he cried timidly, batting his eyelids like an errant lass.

I reached for my bow and in a moment had it strung and then there was another hushed moment as I gently extracted a shaft from my quiver and I could see that he knew, knew that I felt in no generous mood towards those who had hampered my journey, and in the terrified look on his face was the realization that, as sure as I would fondle and play with a maiden that night, he— SCUM—would die.

He rose to his feet, turned and began to run.

I let fly the shaft. It hit him on the back of the head and broke open his skull and, stepping nearer, I watched as the blood gurgled from the vaginal wound.

"Who would have thought that such a meager fellow could have so much blood?"

Three

The next morning I breezed over to the office and loaded my car up with stock. I had decided to run the goods up to Taos instead of sending them by mail. There were a few places I could hit along the way and a few other places up there. I could usually make sales better in person than over the phone, though of course there was a hell of a lot more running around. But when people saw the merchandise, felt it between their fingers, they often bought what they wouldn't over the phone.

George gave me five dollars for gas. I put nine gallons in the tank, got a container of coffee and a glazed donut, and, after stuffing my wallet in the glovebox, headed north.

Putting my wallet in the glovebox was a habit with me. As soon as I got in the car, I always put my wallet there, and as soon as I was getting out, I'd retrieve it, because I hated the feel of the wallet pushing up against my behind when I drove.

I went by a roadside trading company about ten miles outside of town that sold all sorts of tourist junk, and they were closed, but twenty miles further on, in

Española, I had some luck at a place called Tito's Rock Shop. I got him to buy seventy-five arrowheads and a couple of wolf skulls, which put me in good spirits. My commission was only four dollars and seventy cents, but it was a start.

I drove with the windows rolled down and the radio on loud, keeping the needle steadily at ten miles above the speed limit. There were some shut up fruit stands along the side of the road and then I entered the canyon, cliffs rising up to my right. To my left, down below, the Rio Grande, sliding along towards Albuquerque and Las Cruces, and then Mexico, where all the polygamists would wade over from Texas to have sex and shoot each other with shotguns.

There were a few small towns through there, with populations of ten or twenty, but nothing worth bothering with, and I was soon edging out and the vista opened up to me, that vast expanse cracked in the middle by the gorge and in the distance high, solemn mountains.

I got to Taos at about a quarter after eleven. It was not a big town, but was a main stop on the tourist circuit and so did a fair trade. It was an old Indian village that had been conquered by the Spanish and later got over-run by lesbian painters and lecherous poets who could be heard humping in the bushes. I guess that's what attracted the longhairs to the place, and probably more grass was sold in town than anything else.

But right away I really knocked one out of the park. I had put a couple of high-ticket items in the car, such as a few Acoma pots, an Iroquois mask, and some kachina dolls, not thinking I'd be able to sell them, but figuring it never hurt to try.

I toted them and a bunch of other goods into Guajardo's, on the Plaza, which was the biggest such shop in town. There was an old wagon, probably from the 1800's, on the roof, that would catch anyone's eye, and the windows were full of pottery and necklaces.

I was taking stuff out of the box and showing them to him, and he was shaking his head, when a lady walked in. She was dressed garishly in rhinestone jeans, cowboy hat and boots that looked like they had been manufactured that morning. My eyes instinctively swept over her hands and saw the rock she was wearing on her finger which looked like it must have been some sort of De Beers showpiece.

Guajardo grinned at her and asked her if she needed any help. She pouted unenthusiastically and waggled around the shop for a few minutes and then her eyes fell on one of the kachina dolls I had brought in.

"What's *that*?" she asked

"That, ma'am," I said, "is a genuine Hopi Indian early morning singer kachina doll."

"What's it made of?"

"It's carved from the sacred cottonwood root."

"It's beautiful!"

Guajardo was about to say something, but I didn't give him the chance.

"That's right," I said. "It's a sacred Indian spirit that is said to bring good luck to the owner, especially when it comes to matters of fertility. Look at the fine lines and just imagine the patience involved in making it. You can see effort and talent in every stroke."

"You sure can. It would look wonderful over my mantle in Houston," she said.

She asked how much it was and next thing I knew Guajardo had me in the back room talking business.

"How much do you want for it?" he asked.

"Well it would retail for two hundred and forty dollars."

"I didn't ask how much it would retail for, I asked how much *you* want for it."

I told him that I wanted one hundred and eighty berries.

"But that's only a twenty-five percent discount!"

"It's a guaranteed sale."

"I can sell her something else."

"Maybe so, maybe not. Once one of these folks gets themselves set on something it can be pretty hard to switch them to something else. She's squirming in her pants for that kachina doll, but if she doesn't get it, she'll probably just go somewhere else and look for one like it."

He scratched his ear and saw my point.

He ended up selling her the doll for two hundred and seventy-five dollars though, so still made out pretty good.

After the transaction was complete, I went over to a place called Twelve Winds and managed to sell them a few spearheads and rattles and a beaded breastplate choker.

My total sales for the day were now three hundred and one dollars and my commission was thirty dollars and ten cents, and I still hadn't got to Christine's.

I looked at my watch. It was twelve fifty-five and I was hungry. The only thing I had eaten all day had been the donut.

I was doing so well that I decided to treat myself to lunch over at the Taos Inn and sat at the bar and ordered the chicken taco plate and a margarita. The drink came first and I swallowed it down and found it refreshing enough to order a second which came just as the tacos did. I loaded them up with salsa and they were delicious. I wolfed down the first two quick and was half way through the third when some joker came and parked himself near me. He was wearing a white short-sleeve shirt, white shorts, brand new white tennis shoes and had pale, thin, wobbly legs and a mouth full of false teeth.

"Whisky and a splash," he told the bartender, and as he reached for his drink I noticed that he wore a wrist watch the silver band of which was studded with about a pound of turquoise. I figured it must have cost him at least three bills.

"Nice timepiece you got there," I said.

He turned deliberately on his stool to face me.

"It's Zuni sleeping beauty turquoise," he said in the slow concise speech of an upper-class alky.

I gave him a phony smile. "It's a superb piece of jewelry," I said.

"I'm a collector. Taos school. I got nineteen paintings. I go in for the rugs and pots too. The simplicity of Bert Geer Phillips just floors me."

"You like Native American crafts?"

"Oh, yes. Pueblo pottery. Shamanistic items. The diurnal rotation of feathers and clay."

I swallowed down the last of my taco and told him not to move. He didn't. I went out to my car, opened the trunk and, after looking through some junk, found what I wanted. It was a pipe made from a deer antler and decorated with feathers, beads and thongs and had a medicine bag attached to it. A guy down in Socorro made them for us at five bucks each and gave them an aged look by soaking them in urine and burying them in his back yard for a month.

I returned, sat down and handed it to him.

"That's a quality artifact," I told him.

"I believe you." His hands were shaking a little as he held it.

I decided to lay it on thick.

"I'm not sure how old it is, but when I acquired it I was told that it belonged to Old Chief Smoke, which would place it about 1850. But I doubt it was new even when he had it."

"Old Chief Smoke? When I was nine years old I saw his body on display at the Smithsonian Institute." His false teeth sort of jiggled around in his mouth. "How much would you, um, be inclined to part with this rarity for?"

"Part with it? Gee, it had never occurred to me to sell it. I just figured that you, being a collector and all, could appreciate looking at it."

He sighed. "I can," he said, "I certainly can."

He had the pipe in one hand and reached for his drink with the other. I could see the hoops in his mind waving around.

"Of course I cannot blame you for your desire to retain the object," he sympathized. "But it is a cultural artifact and must be safeguarded against deterioration. One has to know how to handle such things and, you must understand, I would take good care of it and preserve it for future generations. The babies of today are the men of tomorrow. Upon my demise, everything of cultural value that I own will go to the Wilbur T. Davis Museum of the Americas."

"Yeah, then maybe you *would* be a better person to have it than me."

"Better is too conclusive a word. But tell me, if you were to, um, transfer this item to my care, what remuneration would you expect?"

"Well, I bought it for two hundred and ninety dollars, and I certainly couldn't be expected to sell it for less than that."

"Indeed not. I would neither expect nor desire such a disadvantageous outcome for an individual as excellent as yourself."

"Yeah, I really never thought of selling it, but seeing as you're an experienced collector, and seeing that the piece would eventually be there for future generations to admire and study—well, what do you think about three hundred and ten dollars? I realize that the twenty dollars profit on my part might seem a little greedy but, as I said, my intentions were to keep the item for myself."

He reached for his drink, blinked a few times and then took a long swallow. Then he turned, opened his eyes wide and looked into mine.

"I will buy this!" he said.

"Yeah?"

"I will buy this!"

He was a nice guy and pulled out his wallet. He must have had about four hundred dollars cash in it, and counted three hundred and ten out to me and then told the bartender to set us up with a couple more drinks on him and that he wanted to take care of my whole bill as well.

We parted ways twenty minutes later, me offering him a generous handshake, and him still grasping the pipe tightly in his left hand.

When I got to Christine's Curiosity Shop, it was already past two o'clock.

She had all sorts of junk everywhere, everything from framed daguerreotypes to old derringers. A stuffed owl sat on top of an upside-down coil basket. An old Apache cradleboard hung next to a painting of a cowboy and his dog, the latter resembling a panda bear more than anything else.

Her shop was full of curiosities all right, but she was probably the most curious thing in there. I'm not sure how old she was, but I doubted she was much younger than me. She must have weighed in at about one-eighty and the top of her head came up to the bottom of my chin. She had dusty pink lipstick on and her mouth looked nice.

Though she had plenty of junk in her shop, I guess she wanted more. She ended up buying what she had asked for on the phone plus, with just the slightest pressure from myself, a couple of Sioux style pipebags at eight bucks a shake.

"You in a hurry?" she asked after she had written out a check.

"I guess not."

"Good, because if there's one thing I like it's a man who knows how to take it slow."

She closed up her shop and we went upstairs to her kitchenette apartment. She tossed on a Todd Rundgren record and poured a couple shots of tequila which we drank off before embracing. It wasn't the most romantic event of my life, but I had had worse fun too.

Four

It was the best day of sales I had had since being with George. I had done three hundred and ninety-seven dollars, which gave me a commission of thirty-nine dollars and seventy cents. And that wasn't including the deer antler pipe, which I had no intention of telling George about. Including that, my total day's take was three hundred and forty-nine dollars and seventy cents.

When I got back to Santa Fe, I stopped over at Kaune's, a grocery store around the corner from my house, and picked up a pound of ground chuck, a pack of meat franks, a pound package of spiced luncheon meat, a pound of sharp cheddar cheese, a couple of onions, a dozen white tortillas, a loaf of white bread, a quart of mayonnaise, a can of fruit cocktail, a 1-lb can of Folgers coffee, a 10-oz jar of Maxwell House instant coffee, a deck of Benson & Hedges, a six-pack of ginger ale, a six-pack of Falstaff, and a bottle of Pinch, dying of thirst someone once said something about hell or swimming around in one's own juice I almost felt like it but didn't you're doing all right. Just keep it up ahead of the game a few rounds between the white posts some wet world.

"That'll be sixteen seventy-three," the cashier said.

To call her pretty would have been like calling Mickey Rooney tall, but she had two globes that looked like they would have been interesting to navigate and, as I handed her a hundred-buck bill, I asked her what time she got off work. She counted me back my change and told me I could ask her boyfriend.

"He's a lucky guy," I said, shoving the change in my pants pocket and thinking that he was lucky all right—about as lucky as a dope fiend in a convent.

I put the groceries on the front seat of the Buick, popped my wallet in the glovebox, and swung over to my street.

Well, it wasn't so much a street as about three hundred feet of dirt with a few broken down houses on one side and the back wall of the Public Service Company of New Mexico power plant on the other. It was a dead end and I lived at the end of it. My house was an old adobe with the stucco flaking off the outside, so the place looked like hell. Inside wasn't much better. A humble kitchen with a table; living-dining room, coffee table, a few bean bag chairs Yvonne had given me, a beat-up sofa and a television that had stopped working six months previously. When I had first taken the place, I had convinced the landlord, Don Steadman, to give me a reduction in rent if I did some fixing up. I hadn't and so the roof still leaked and for that matter I hadn't paid the rent in five months.

When I pulled up to the house I saw a white Ford pickup truck there and sighed. It belonged to Don Steadman. I thought about backing out, but he had already seen me and was getting out and walking over.

He had a sort of doughy face. He was about five years older than me and six inches taller and was wearing cowboy boots, jeans and a checkered shirt.

He came right up to the car door and I got out and put on as big a smile as my face could muster.

"Don," I said, "I've been looking for you."

"I bet."

"I went by your place last week and you weren't there."

"I always thought of myself as pretty easy to find."

"I wanted to get you all that back rent."

"Ever heard of a stamp?"

He wanted to be funny so I laughed.

"You know me," I said. "I don't trust the federal post office with money—even a check. Anyhow, I was waiting around, but had some tickets to the rodeo and——"

"I hate the rodeo, Mitch. Too many horses' asses. Every time I try to get my rent, is all I get is curve balls. But, as far as I'm concerned, things are down to the wire. You can't keep moving the goal posts. I need to get that money, Mitch."

"Sure you do, Don," I said. "Everyone needs money, and you own the place so, sure you're entitled to that back rent."

I saw that he was looking around the front yard. There were waist-high pig-weeds everywhere, an old tire and some other junk. I had to admit that I hadn't been keeping things as tidy as I could have.

"So, you were saying that you have the rent?"

"Yes, I do—well, did—well, do, sort of."

He was looking at the bags of groceries on the car seat, and I could tell that he thought that if I had money to eat and buy the bottle of Pinch that was sticking out of the top of one of the bags, I should have money to pay the rent.

I fished in my pocket and got out the change from the shopping, and counted him out sixty.

"There's rent in advance for July," I said.

"Like hell it is," he said, taking the bills. "This'll go towards the three hundred you owe me. As for July, well, if you don't come up with every penny that you owe me by the end of the month, plus rent in advance for July itself, I'm going to have to get you off the premises. As you know, I've got two sons bigger than myself who would like nothing better than to come over here and help me throw you out. We won't bother calling the police. We'll just throw you out. When you first took the place I wanted eighty dollars and you talked me down to sixty saying you'd make up the other twenty in work on the place. You said you were going to fix the roof, patch the walls, and everything else. You even told me you would plant flowers. Instead of looking better though, you've let it go all to hell. I'd be lucky if I could rent it for fifty now."

Don climbed in his truck and drove off and I got my wallet out of the glovebox and took the groceries in. I didn't like the fact that I had let him get away with sixty dollars, but I figured it was a lot better than him emptying the entire contents of my wallet.

After setting down the groceries on the kitchen table, I went to the freezer for ice. There were two trays. One of them had one cube in it, and the other two, so I knocked them into a glass, filled up the trays with water and stuck them back in the freezer. There was still about half a bottle of Yellowstone, so I sloshed some over the ice cubes then added some ginger ale.

I drank the first ball off quick, then made another, with the ice that was still in my glass, that I planned on nursing.

I unloaded my groceries and then chopped up an onion and put it in a pan with some oil and powdered red chile and let it all sizzle around for a while and then threw in the ground chuck. By this time my second drink was gone, but the new ice wasn't ready yet, so I poured myself a long one and grated the cheddar cheese and let the meat cook and then dumped about half of it in a tortilla, added some cheddar cheese, and went to the table and ate. I was hungry and ate and thought about Don and the rent.

Sure I could have paid him off the whole amount if I had dug into my wallet, but I was glad that I hadn't. I actually regretted giving him what I had. If he was going to come by with his sons on the first of July, the thing to do would be to get out before then. It was the nineteenth of June, and that gave me a good week and a half to find something. If I needed to I could rent a room at the Hotel St. Francis downtown. It was true that it was mostly just a bunch of old men sitting around waiting for government checks, but it would do until I found something better.

The main thing was to be stepping up in life.

I started thinking that maybe the Indian artifacts line wasn't so bad. A guy could pick a lot of berries. The problem was that George was going about it ass back-wards. He was out there trying to drum up as many arrowhead sales as possible, when the real money was in the high-ticket items. Sure, the arrowheads were worth doing for a little pocket change, but one high-ticket item could bring in as much money as selling a thousand of those damned arrowheads.

I dragged the bottle of Yellowstone into the living room, sat down on the couch and poured myself another drink, a short one this time, and was just starting to feel pretty well oiled. I looked at my weights on the floor. I hadn't lifted them since I moved into the place. And that was two years before. One of these days I would give myself a good workout, but this wasn't it.

There was the Zenith black and white nineteen-inch, but it wasn't going to miraculously start working on its own. I needed to either get it fixed or get rid of it. And there was a telephone that was plugged in but had been disconnected for some time.

Living in a world in which nothing worked, everything was on stand-still, waiting for when I could get up out of the dust. Thank God I had the Buick.

I looked at my watch. It was nine.

I thought about swinging over to the Art Cinema X on Cerrillos and St. Francis, to catch *Love Rites in Denmark*, which they would be doing continuous showings of until midnight, but I had already seen it a few times so decided to skip it.

There was the can of fruit cocktail, but I was pretty full and decided to save it for later.

I had about a dozen skin mags on the coffee table and picked up a copy of *Cavalier*.

I leafed through it for a bit admiring the photography and then came across an article titled "Are Plump Girls Best in Bed?" that I read, though admittedly without much interest since I figured I had already had one lesson on the subject that day.

There was a knock on the door.

I decided it was probably Yvonne looking for a little of what I had given her the night before. I didn't really want to see her. But the lights were on and if I didn't get the door she'd probably just let herself in, since it wasn't locked. I decided that I would let her go climb into my bed for a while, but not spend the night. We'd rub up against each other and there would be some turmoil and then I'd send her home.

I hoisted myself to my feet and opened the door.

A young man was standing there. In one hand he had a book and what looked like a folded up street map. He was standing there staring at me and at first I didn't say hello and neither did he.

"Can I help you?" I finally asked.

"I don't know. Can you?"

His voice had a whiney quality to it. His hair was brown and his small eyes were frosty blue. He had a very white face, pimples screwing everything, thin lips, and a cleft in his chin. He was wearing jeans, a long-sleeve button-down shirt, and a pair of brown Padrino oxfords.

"I think you've got the wrong house," I told him.

"Is your name Mitch Mazzola?"

"Yeah."

"Then I don't have the wrong house."

"Look," I said, "whatever you're selling, I don't want it. If you're here to collect money—I don't have it. If you want something else, spill, or get lost."

"I'm your son," he said flatly.

"Like hell you are."

"If you're Mitch Mazzola, then I'm your son. My name is Calvin. You *made love* to my mother."

A kind of cold feeling came over me. My mind jumped backward and forward, knowing damned well what he was saying but not wanting to understand and pretty sure that it must have been a con of some sort; but then all the women, winding and squirming, and how could I possibly remember them all, their cries of joy, their satisfied laughter wet sheaths but didn't always use them moaning pleasure always willing to pay for half an abortion? Was there a chance that it was true?

"I guess I should invite you in," I finally said.

"I guess you should."

I looked around but didn't see a vehicle.

"Where's your car?" I asked.

"I walked," he said.

He stepped in and looked around. His eyes fell on the skin magazine and the bottle of booze and he blinked a few times.

"You want a drink?"

"Okay."

He followed me into the kitchen. I checked the ice and it was ready. I could have probably milked two more drinks from the bottle of Yellowstone in the living room, but went ahead and opened the bottle of Pinch instead, fixed us a couple of highballs with that and shoved one of them into his hand.

He took a sip and didn't seem too happy with the taste. I couldn't help but think that I was wasting good liquor. He wasn't exactly the kind of drinking companion I wanted.

We sat down at the table and looked at each other. He studied my face and I studied his. His features were neat, almost feminine. If you had put a wig on him he would have looked almost cute. His hands were fine and white and looked like the hardest work they had done was wiping his own ass.

"So what's the story?" I asked.

"Does the name Claudia Ralston mean anything to you?"

I told him, quite honestly, that it didn't.

"That's my mother's name, so it's no surprise that for you it's meaningless. I asked her about you—lots of times. At first she lied and said you were an army captain and died in the Battle of Pork Chop Hill, but finally she told me the truth."

"Which is?"

"I'm twenty years old, so you do the math. That one night she met you in the bar of the La Fonda and you fed her drinks." He held up his hand. "You seduced her and she never saw you again."

He made me nervous.

"If she was pregnant she should have come looking for me," I said.

"Maybe she did."

I swallowed off my drink and poured a nice belt of whisky over the ice that was left in the glass. He took a sip of his, put it down pushing her oily body up tried to imagine him as a woman as he leaned back and grinned. There was something about him I didn't exactly like—well, a lot about him I didn't like, someone coming over at night and laying a heavy trip like that on me. I felt like he probably didn't respect me as a man and probably figured he was better than me.

I thought back. I had laid an awful lot of women in my time. When I was younger as many as three a day. Twenty-one years ago. The bar of the La Fonda. Yeah, I had definitely done some scouting there. A girl with a plain face and an elaborate necklace, a tall married woman with high cheekbones, some little tramp from Texas who squealed like a pig, or the whimpering sounds of those with faces I couldn't remember, panties and pantyhose flying everywhere and bras springing around. What would I do with him? Give him some titty and a sudden intuition of firm white thighs crossed my mind and the feeling that I had been doing her a favor.

"This is all pretty sudden," I told Calvin.

"Less sudden for me."

"You just wanted to see what I looked like?"

"I never really thought about it. But you probably looked better when you were younger. My mother lives in town you know."

"Yeah?"

"Yeah—I can't—I don't want to stay with her anymore."

"So, what is it that you *do* want?"

He shrugged his shoulders and frowned.

"Do you have some place to go?" I asked.

"If I did I wouldn't have come here. I don't have any friends in town—not any real friends. I was, um, educated out of state. Maybe my mother never wanted me to see you. Maybe she felt ashamed. If I were her I would have. And never having a real home, I never had a chance to, um, bond with other boys."

"A loner, huh?"

He didn't reply but just stared at me.

"I'm kind of a loner myself," I said, as if apologizing.

I told him to follow me and we went into the living room. I opened the closet and pulled out an old White Stag sleeping bag I had and told him he could sleep on the sofa. I wondered if I should put my hand on his shoulder but decided not to. I really didn't like the idea of him sleeping there, but didn't see that I had much of a choice.

I lay on my bed in my underwear and smoked a cigarette and nursed a ball.

I couldn't figure out if the kid was bulling me or not. But his story didn't sound all that implausible. He didn't look much like me—at all. But he did have a cleft in his chin. And what would he gain by searching me out and lying? It was clear enough that I didn't have much to offer him in the way of amenities.

He was twenty. I had first come to town around twenty-three years earlier, from Alamogordo, where I had been working at a five-and-dime store. I had had a girlfriend named Tracy, a hot little dish with a snub nose, who needed to come up to Santa Fe to attend her cousin's wedding. Well, there were a few cases of cold duck and everyone was pretty high and next thing I knew

I was in the bathroom with an extra-leggy redhead and the door was locked.

Tracy yelled a little and cried a lot and returned to Alamogordo by herself. I stayed and had the time of my life. There were just too many nice women to get into to have to stay with one. I sure did prowl the bars back then. Well, I prowled more than the bars. I'd pick up women at grocery stores, laundromats, cafeterias, pancake breakfasts, while standing in line at the bank, at patio sales or church bazaars. Admittedly I was better looking then—or at least a tiny bit more fit.

That went on for a couple of years and then I headed out to California. To San Jose, where I worked as a gigolo. Those were good days and there was plenty of gratification. Usually it was married women who wanted my services. They would have me meet them at hotels and throw inhibition to the wind.

"Thank you so much!"

"I was only doing my job."

"You sure know how to work."

"It feels good?"

"Oh, honey, you know it does!"

As strange as it may seem, usually the ones that paid for it were more beautiful than the ones who I didn't charge. But all the girls wanted me, rich or poor, fat or slim. They could smell the manhood that oozed out of me.

"Just one more time, Mitch! Kiss me, Mitch, kiss me now! Do it like you mean it! It's a perfect fit! I want to eat you up, Mitch! You're such a GOOD-LOOKER! Let me be your slave! Oh, Mitch! I'll leave my husband for you!

I'll leave my boyfriend for you! Let's go to Tijuana and have sex on the beach! I NEVER KNEW IT COULD BE LIKE THIS!!!"

I was making more dough than I knew what to do with. I lived on nothing but steak and champagne. There was a polar bear skin rug on the floor of my apartment and I had a pair of Siamese kittens. I took my garments to a French stripper who would clean them in exchange for kisses.

Of course, having so many women friends meant that men naturally didn't like me.

"Come on, Mitch, you can hook me up."

"Not everyone can do my line of work."

"But I'm telling you, I'll work for FREE!"

"No can do. My clients expect a certain quality, a quality only I can deliver."

And boy did I deliver. Day after day, night after night. Weeks followed one on the next, naked flesh sprawled open before me. I was like an acrobat, risking my life everyday on the high-wire of love.

"You're under arrest."

"For what?"

"Prostitution."

"But I'm a man!"

I travelled north, to another California city, and rented a second story apartment in the tenderloin. For the first time I started allowing clients up to my place—a modest number at first, really, but then the crowd grew. Word must have got out where they could have a good time. My address must have been scribbled in half the ladies' lavatories around town. They would bring me gifts—flowers, cologne, silk ties, and diamond cufflinks. Sometimes they would cook me breaded pork chops or make me salads with vinaigrette dressing. I had to have four mattresses just to keep up with the traffic. It got so that I could hardly sleep.

The crisis came when I met, um, Debbie Atherton. She was not only a certified nymphomaniac, but also the wife of an assistant DA. She would pay me generously and always give me little things, like chocolate-covered cherries or golf sweaters. She came over at 7:05 on a Wednesday night saying that her husband was out of town and she could play as late as she wanted. She had brought a quart of Echo Springs and a Boston cream cake and asked me to fix drinks while she went into the bathroom and changed. She came out in a nylon robe and it was a hot evening so we went out on the balcony and started drinking and talking and touching each other, and next thing I knew the robe was open and she was there against the railing and we were doing what we were supposed to be doing. Only I guess we got a little carried away, because she was clawing and gasping and I was telling her how beautiful she was and then she wasn't there at all. I looked over the railing and saw her sprawled out on the sidewalk down below. Luckily she only ended up breaking an arm, but as they were loading her up in the ambulance she started yelling at me, saying that she'd get her husband to indict me for assault and some other things. The cops were asking a lot of questions and the neighbors were giving a lot of answers and I had to split out of town.

I guess it shouldn't really have surprised me that I had a kid. Hell, I probably had twenty or thirty—kids all over the place, from all walks of life and every color of the rainbow. Half Japanese kids and kids with Russian names. Kids reduced to purse snatching or cleaning car windows on the streets of Los Angeles or Phoenix or New Orleans—a whole crowd of them gathering at my door asking for my blessings.

I stubbed out my cigarette and closed my eyes.

I could hear Calvin in the next room, snoring softly.

He was a strange one. I wouldn't have been surprised if he turned out to be a little fay.

Five

Soon, in the distance, I saw the outline of the walls of Oghris and, just as the sun was lowering its burnt copper head over the western moraine, was passing through its great gates.

Leading the mule, I made my way to the bazaar. Slimy beggars waved their hands, expressionless sandstone faces beating before me and lascivious whores whose bodies were smeared with purple paint, whose tongues darted out of their smiling lips, came tapping at my fleshy loins. Scriveners probably queers the smell of sage and entrail readers offered their services. There were dealers in camels and dealers in kirtles. Soon, however, I found what I wanted—a merchant in hides—a wily-looking chap standing before an immense array of animal skins.

"I have hides a-plenty," I told the merchant. "I have hides of wolves and hides of bears and even a thick pelt of the great wooly mammoth."

"I want none of your mammoth hides, for they have gone sorely out of fashion, but I will give you a pittance for the rest."

"A pittance is not a bargain I heed. You must pay with good silver coin, for know that ye have not a knave to deal with, but Mulvizeg the Hunter, he of much misty fame. These hides I bring you are not the stale, moldy sort that lie piled behind you—the hides of felched cats and gnawed-at dogs soiled with old egg yolk and green spittle—but fresh hides from the Sverig Mountains, hides fit for princes and kings."

The merchant replied with an oath and then a toothy grin. "You rascal. Though your form has a mighty appearance, your wits are as sharp as a steel dagger. For though normally mighty men are dim between the ears, you belay this with your cunning. Unload ye here them hides and twenty bright silver coins shall I give ye—but please refrain from dispossessing yourself of yon wooly mammoth hide, for in truth it would be easier to sell the hair off a leper's foot than such a monstrosity as that."

I sighed, thinking of all the trouble I had had in killing the wooly mammoth. I had chased it everywhere and the beast just hadn't wanted to die, though I had asked it nicely and I was piercing it with shaft after shaft, driving them hard and everywhere dancing around in a circle cruelly into it, but some animals DON'T LIKE TO BE EXCITED but we made the deal and right then a big girl with a Wymffrian accent came and started feeling up the bear hides wanting to roll in them.

With purse full of coin I, Mulvizeg, decided that it was time to enjoy the delights of the city, for a night of revelment and a bed of plush down I sore needed after the hardships of the summer hunt.

I strode through the alleys and lanes, leading my mule in jovial wonderment, and they had beads and earrings gazing at sweetmeats and the jiggling breasts with a feather in her hair and she starts painting and I was gazing at the stomachs of passing wantons. Soon I came upon a well-lit tavern and gave up my mule to a filthy though handsome stableboy, with everything unshaven and untrimmed, and I ordered that the beast be given abundant hay and he kissed it and said he would, and then I made my way through the door of the tavern.

The place was noisy with tipsy merriment. Cackling, stomping feet in vagabond boots, bare breast of wolf woman. Smoke hung in the air and my nostrils were assailed by the aroma of cooked meat. Loose ladies sat on the laps of men with long hair and leering lips, feeding them roasted elk and rich wine and kissing them on their throats and beneath their headbands. A little table was just then being vacated, and I pushed myself towards it and took a stool.

"What can I get you, my comely fellow?" a barmaid asked me.

Her eyelashes bobbed up and down.

Her hair was the red color of almandine and she had breasts the size of hatching dragon eggs and it had been long indeed since I had seen such an attractive member of the softer sex. I grabbed her around the waist and pulled her close and in a bantering and seductive tone ordered a pitcher of mead and a trencher of meat and a bed for the night. Soon the food and beverage were before me. I drank deeply and ripped at the meat with my puissant jaws.

"Might I sit here near ye, good sir?"

I looked up. A fat-faced man stood there, wishing to sit with me in the crowded tavern and I did hope indeed that the empty seat was all he wished for and not to splash me with fruit-flavored massage oil or encroach on my evident manhood with obscene and inappropriate looks like some sleazy peeper.

"Seat yourself, and be of good cheer."

His fingers were encumbered by costly rings and his weak legs sheathed in silken hose and about his shoulders hung a cape of finest fur and he had a dainty pout to his lips and to the barmaid lisped out an order for wine and naught else.

"Your cape is a pretty thing," said I.

He turned deliberately on his stool to face me.

"That it is, for it is made from the hide of mountain puma."

I smiled. "It's a fine hide," I said.

"Would I wear other? For I am Cynwrig, Groom of the Stool to Lord Zarkov, and must dress in hide finest."

I took a deep draft of my mead and my mind, becoming suddenly fleet, formed a roguish and clever idea, like if I could just get her panties off while leaving her pants on—I mean, so I told Cynwrig not to move a hair's distance and he didn't and, heaving myself from my seat, I went out to my faithful mule who was in the fast embrace of the stableboy and got the wooly mammoth hide and returned with it.

"Look ye here at this hide," I said, tossing it leisurely on Cynwrig's skinny lap.

The Groom of the Stool blinked twice and then ran his delicate hands over the pelt with questioning admiration.

"It is large and thick!"

(Would it be any other way?)

"It is a rare specimen," said I, Mulvizeg the Hunter.

"A specimen of what, pray tell?"

"It, good man, is nothing less than the hide of the Giant Ermine of the Sverig Mountains!"

"Giant Ermine? Be is there such a thing?"

"Then ye have not read deep in your lore. For even the snarling saber-toothed tigers dare not approach the giant ermines of the Sverig Mountains, who are, it is known, to be the very pets of the God Ogroth, and it is with their skin he makes his bed and on this he amuses himself with and dehymenates the nymphs and dryads and the worse he would treat them the more they would like him and he would handle their feet and some older ones smelled like armpits—but he didn't need to gamble or worry, because with the giant ermine pelt you would be the most fashionable man in all of Oghris."

"You don't say?"

"It is as I say and as thou shalt discover should ye make this hide thine!"

"And how much would such a fine skin cost?" he asked.

"I could not part with it for less than three gold coins."

"Then it is three gold coins ye shall have, for I dare say it is a bargain at that price!"

And with these words he unburdened his purse of this weight, the three golden moons rolling into my strong palm.

I drank many drafts with Cynwrig, all at the latter's expense, and together we sang of miscreant love and the joys of sin. Then, after laughing ten thousand laughs and praising me, Mulvizeg the Hunter, many times and patting me on the knee, the Groom of the Stool rose up and took his leave, clutching his newly bought hide and stumbling out the door.

I finished the mead in my cup, wiped my stalwart chin and then called to the barmaid, who came bouncing up with a saucy smile and she had a wild look in her eyes like, um, she wanted to be alone with me and LET ME DO ANYTHING THAT I WANTED TO HER STOMACH AND BREASTS AND HAIR.

"Come good miss, show me to my chamber!"

A moment later we were standing at the door of a small but clean room, furnished with nothing more than a piss pot shaped like a ghost and a four-poster bed that was decked with blankets and extra large fluffy pillows embroidered with nude female athletes.

I unbuckled my sword and leaned it against the wall, then turned towards the barmaid and looked at her strongly. Whether it was the mead or the flickering light of the candle she held, I know not, but she looked more enticing and ripe than any fruit I had ever witnessed, low-hanging fruit that she was.

"Ye *are* a handsome creature."

"And ye have pretty eyes," she said.

"It is not just my eyes that are pretty!!!"

"Are ye trying to woo me?" she asked. "When first I saw ye I knew that ye would make my body thine own."

"Do ye think this to be my wish?"

She laughed wildly as she unburdened herself of cloth-ing, flashing at me the raw frankness of her bosom.

"Show me your lustihood, hunter," she said, pushing herself up against my brawn, "for your presence speaks of amatory skill and sentimental excitement."

The bed crunched under our weight.

She panted out a few desperate words as she offered me her nakedness. Her body was cloud-soft, her legs like a vise. I grabbed at her pearl whiteness, straining the cords of my muscles as if I were struggling with a famished she lion, the sound ripping through the air flocks of crows beating their wings over jagged spear tips increasing in tempo us improvising like dusted mime artists limbs moving in exotic sweaty sign language screaming discordant notes of pleasure spraying the air happy as flower people tapping out intricate patterns of lust.

I had not had a dame-companion in many moons and it took much to satiate my desire. Her gratification she expressed in countless ways, now swaying her body over me, now thrusting it beneath and begging to be smote without mercy and then the bed began to jump about and seemed as if it was going to be driven right through the floor, is it because your mom raised ye on her own, is that why ye don't have any friends? He plays by himself, but he's a good boy. A good boy?

"Good, good, *good*, good . . . g-ooo-ddddd! *Good!* Goooooooooood . . ."

Dawn found me, Mulvizeg the Hunter, stretched nude upon the bed. The barmaid was gone, but as a sign of her gratification she had left on her pillow a single white rose.

I picked it up and inhaled deeply. The smell was gorgeous, reminding me not only of the thrilling palpitations of the night before, but also of the old lusts of my lascivious pilgrimages to a million brothels thirty new females a day, earthly and carnal and sensual and she was walking towards me and I could tell she wasn't wearing a bra.

There was a sudden pounding at the door and I wondered if word had not gone out through the city that there was one skilled in the art of seduction and maybe there were now other dames lined up outside, panting to be mastered in a firm way.

I covered my groin with a pillow.

"Come in!" I cried.

A lean young man stood with arms akimbo at the door.

"Are you Mulvizeg the Hunter?"

"I am he."

"Then it is to ye that I wish to speak."

"Why for?"

"For I, bold sir, am none other than your son, Ruaidh-rigo, lost to you through time and circumstance, come to reclaim my patronymic!!!"

Six

The next morning when I woke up, Calvin had coffee all ready. It was strong as hell, but tasted good and, after slugging down a couple of cups, I headed for the door.

"Where are you going?"

"Work."

"You work?"

"Yeah, at A-1 Relics and Curios, and I'm already late. See you tonight. If you're still here."

"I will be."

I guess I should have felt glad that he would be. A son. But I didn't. I had enough to worry about without some jerk kid coming and latching on to me. I figured, just as a matter of principle, I'd let him stay for a day or two if he wanted. But then I'd give him the old heave-ho. It was hard enough carrying my own weight, let alone that of some young man in search of emotional fulfillment.

As I pulled out of my street, I looked at my watch. It was exactly ten.

I wondered if I should swing by Horacio's and get a quick one on my way in, but decided against it. I was already running late and George might smell it on my breath and I didn't want him to think I was a lush. The job was crap, but it was a job. And I needed to start drinking less anyhow. Time to make some money and get back in shape.

I figured me telling George about the sales from the day before would put him in a good mood. I wouldn't tell him about all of the sales of course. The peace pipe had been my deal and had been paid for with cash, so I would keep that a secret. If I could get another day like that before the end of the month though, I'd be set to move into a nice little furnished place somewhere.

I took the boxes of unsold goods out of the trunk, lugged them up the stairs and opened the door. When I walked in George was gazing at me from his desk. He looked like he was about to cry. I could tell something was wrong. I set the boxes down on the floor and walked over, grinning.

"I need honest people in my organization, Mitch."

The grin left my face. "I am honest."

"You might be, but that bottle that's got hold of you isn't."

"I'm not sure I know what you're referring to, George."

"Day before yesterday, when I went out for the hamburger sandwiches."

"So?"

"You told me there was no business. But thirty minutes ago a guy came in, some slicker from California. Said he had purchased a tomahawk and ten arrowheads on Monday. He wanted ten more arrowheads to give to his nephew in Bakersfield. So I sold them to him."

"Yeah, I was going to tell you about that."

"You didn't put the money in the till. There's even a dollar and eight cents missing."

"I was going to tell you about it," I insisted.

"That doesn't sound like the truth," he said.

"Look, George, I screwed up, okay? I'll admit it. But yesterday I had a hell of a day. I cleared four hundred and eighteen dollars worth of merchandise. You know that old doll that you loaded me up with yesterday? The one you said you wanted a hundred bucks for? Well, I sold it to Guajardo for one-eighty! And on top of that I sold Tito seventy-five arrowheads and some wolf skulls and I sold Christine a couple of pipebags on top of the powder horns and bannerstones!"

I laid the checks and sales receipts down on the desk in front of him. He looked them over and shook his head.

"You're not a bad salesman, Mitch. But dammit."

He pulled a pad of paper over and then started to do some math with a pencil. The telephone rang and I was about to pick it up but he waved me away and picked it up himself.

"Yes. No. Not here. Check the local bar. He'll be down at Horacio's if it's open, I reckon."

He hung up the phone, looked down at the notepad, finished his calculations, and then opened the drawer of his desk and took out the cashbox. He handed me forty-six dollars and thirty-three cents.

"Here, take this," he said. "It's fourteen hours in wages plus your commission minus the twenty-three dollars and ninety-two cents from Monday, though I did include a ten percent commission on that sale—God knows why! I'm also overlooking the one dollar and eight cents that's missing from the cash box. Now, take it and get out."

"Get out?"

"I'm afraid so. Until you get sober at least. You're not a bad man. And, like I said, you're an all right salesman. But all this drinking . . ." He shook his head. "It's making you dishonest, Mitch."

I wanted to yell at him, to tell him what a bastard he was, but I didn't.

I stuffed the money in my pocket, swung around and left the place. Hell, I wouldn't go back if I stopped drinking everything but ice water. I knew damned well that the reason he had fired me had nothing to do with the fact that I had a few beers every now and again. He had fired me because he didn't know how to run a business and he knew that I knew he didn't know how and he was jealous of all those sales I scared up out of the chamisa while he just wandered back and forth to the post office sending little packets of arrowheads to nine year old kids in Dayton, Ohio and Baltimore, Maryland.

I pointed the Buick towards the Plaza and parked there and sat for a while thinking. George said I could be found at Horacio's. Not true. I'd go out and get another job. I'd have one by the end of the day. I was probably one of the most employable men in the Southwest.

I climbed out of the car and got a paper from a vending machine and went over to a bench and started looking through the help wanted ads. Group leader needed for treatment of emotionally disturbed adolescents. Investor needed. Stuff envelopes twenty-five dollars per hundred. Administrative assistant to be right hand of dynamic president of multi-faceted leisure activities business. Oil rig position. Janitor, Church of Holy Light. Part-time clean up boy. Hot tamale maker. Lubricating oil salesmen. Spanish speaking book keeper.

I dragged out a butt and lit it, thinking it might be worth applying for the lubricating oil salesman position, then went to the back of the paper, to the funnies, hoping to read *Prince Valiant*, but he wasn't there—I guess they only put him in on Sundays, and there was only *Pogo* and *Buz Sawyer* and *Steven Canyon*.

Looking around. It was the usual drunks and sleepy old men and men with moustaches and sunglasses, who were probably undercover cops, leaning against the posts of the porticos in front of Dunlaps and JC Penney Co. In the center of the Plaza there was a big phallic piece of stone that had been set there to commemorate the slaughter of a bunch of Indians and beyond that, on the far side of the Plaza, were the dead people's descendents, sitting in front of the Palace of the Governors selling jewelry.

A man and woman came and sat down at a bench about fifteen feet to one side and opposite mine and the woman seemed to have a good shape, though it was a little shy beneath some sort of poly-cotton shift. She was wearing a pair of village tan grasshopper sandals with spaghetti straps and was a delight to look at. When the man turned his head away I smiled at her and she smiled back. I licked my lips thinking that I still had to get a job and about anti-pornography legislation, then when he looked back she became serious again. He was some hollow-chested bastard with a thin moustache smeared above his mouth and he reached over and took her hand.

You'd better hang on to her, I thought.

He noticed me staring at her, sit around naked feeling each other recruiting and at first looked at me hard thinking I would look away, but I didn't. I just took a drag of my cigarette and gazed him down. Finally, he said something to her and they got up and she wagged at me as she went. If she had been alone I would have offered to give her a private massage.

I was smiling but inside didn't feel so great, felt that somewhere along the line I had goofed. Other guys were running around with good jobs and hot and willing women and I hadn't been able to capitalize on my own assets. Have to stay with the offence even if sometimes I did get hit on by a queer, so I sat there for a while longer, looking at the stems of the women as they passed by, not really with interest so much as out of habit, thinking that if I had got as much tail as a metaphysical conversation I had being broke all my life, imagine what I could do if I had money. Instead of just banging to engage in salacious smut these sweaty babes like Yvonne I would have some whoever I wanted, whenever and wherever.

George said I would go to Horacio's. Well, I wasn't going to *not* go just because he said I *would*.

With the money left from the evening before and the forty-six dollars and thirty-three cents George had given me, I had almost three hundred dollars. I could certainly afford a drink or two.

I hoisted myself off the bench and sauntered down West San Francisco Street until I was at the bar. At that hour the place was empty. Horacio was behind the counter, standing there, frozen.

"Shouldn't you be polishing glasses or something?" I asked him.

He ignored the question and set me up with a beer and a shot of George Dickel Tennessee whisky.

The place was not an especially chic establishment, but the drinks were cheaper than anywhere else within shooting distance and there was a pool table in the basement for anyone who could get up enough energy to fall down there.

I nailed myself to the bar and bulled with Horacio a little. I told him a few off-color jokes that he didn't laugh at, so I decided to let him talk for a while, me watching his massive jaw chew on the words before he spit them out, his eyes deadpan as he talked about when he was in the service.

"Sure I was in the war. We had a rough time of it."

"I bet."

"I was in Saipan. It was hot as hell. I looked over and my buddy next to me had red running down his cheek. He fell down dead. I kept going. Then I got up there and raised the flag. The Japs started jumping off the cliff. Into the sea. And I don't mean one or two. They attacked us. Many of them had only bamboo sticks. We kept shooting them and they would fall down dead. After we had shot all the ones that were running, others came—wounded men with arms in slings and bandaged up heads. We told them to stop, but they wouldn't, so we shot them. Hundreds of them were jumping. They'd rather jump off a cliff than let us come near them. I got up there and raised the flag. There wasn't any wind and the cloth just lay there still. I wished a wind would come along and blow it, make it move, but it didn't. But all the same, I had planted that goddamned flag there."

"That must have been quite a feeling," I said.

He nodded his head slowly and walked to the other end of the bar and started fiddling with something and pretending to be busy.

I grinned and took a swallow of my whisky and started wondering if maybe I shouldn't apply for the lubricating oil salesman position. It seemed like it could be lucrative.

I had sold, or tried to sell, just about everything in my time. Magazine subscriptions, metal social security plates, typewriter ribbons. For about a week I was trying to sell FOG-Stop windshield cloths, but in a rainless summer it didn't turn out so well. Then I had done a stint as a shoe salesman and that had been all right, until I was canned for, you guessed it, drinking on the job. Not that I had been drunk. I had just had a few short ones at lunchtime, but the manager of the place was one of those hellfire and brimstone types who figured any kind of drinking was a sin, especially any that happened before sundown. The funny thing was that after that I started trying to sell Hertel Bibles. But if people were buying shoes, they sure as hell weren't buying Bibles, and I guess that fellow knew that it was easier to spout the gospel than to try and make a dime on it.

The job I had had before working for George had been going door to door selling Sweet Dart Cosmetics. The stuff actually sold all right and I would have made out if I hadn't ended up giving half my stock away to women whose panties I wanted to get inside. I guess I earned more tail than cash on that job, which had been okay with me, though less so with everyone I owed money to.

I lit a Benson & Hedges and a large cloud of smoke formed in front of me.

I had figured working for George I could make good money. I knew some of that Indian junk sold for a lot. I had heard of guys making a thousand bucks a week selling Indian artifacts. And judging from how I had done the day before, maybe I could have started getting ahead. But apparently that was not my ultimate destiny and nothing ever seemed to go right for me. And I damned well wasn't getting any younger and now here I was a father with a kid I didn't want and didn't want to see, just because I had let someone shove her titties against me twenty-one years before.

But if I wanted an answer, I had to ask the right questions.

How could I develop my own special abilities have fringe benefits be free from the conflicting demands that other people made of me? Job security? A job that required repeated pushing and bending over? Somewhat hard. Hard. Very hard. A million giggles, to forget that he blew his brains out, money, but it never came easy, so I wanted a job, but didn't want a job—I wanted as much as I deserved—wanted to be somebody, to have even a few thousand dollars, to unzip my pants and take a leak.

I went to the head and when I came back a female was pressed up against the bar two stools down from mine. She wore a pair of red reptile-print pumps. A pink calico top was glued to her breasts and she had on a pair of jeans that were tight everywhere but the hemline. She had bright blue eyes that laughed at me and I undressed her with my own eyes and decided she was probably worth socializing with.

I sat down and said hello.

"My name's Romaine."

"Nice."

"You have one?"

I told her.

She smiled and attached her lips to her drink. She didn't seem too quick, but I sure got the feeling she was easy. She was letting off as much heat as a four-burner stove and I figured is all I had to do was knock and she'd let me in.

I had Horacio set me up again and told him to give the lady another of what she was having.

"Gin and tonic," she said in a voice that was doing its best to sound husky.

There was something about her that turned my dials in the right direction.

"I haven't ever seen you in here before," I said.

"It's because I'm so tiny."

"You don't look that tiny."

"Oh, but I am."

Her clothes told a whole different story. She didn't have a ring on her finger but I didn't ask her about her status. She talked and smiled a lot and drank the drinks I bought her and probably could have made me forget my woes, heart beating faster, bringing on the perspiration, cut the monotony.

"Where are you from?" I asked her.

"What, you don't think I'm from around here?"

"I'd have remembered a smile as nice as yours," I said.

"Yeah?"

"Sure."

"I'm from Arizona. In town for a little visiting my sister. But her place is too small and she's got a kid. So I'm staying over at the Thunderbird Inn. Room twelve."

I sucked at my drink and nodded my head wondering what it would be like to spend a long hot Wednesday in bed with her.

She must have guessed what I was thinking.

"Of course it's not much of a vacation. I keep having to look after my sister's kid. I've got to go there pretty soon, but needed a drink first so I could deal with it."

I understood what she meant. I had a kid at home too and was going to have to deal with him. There seemed to be a few dilemmas in my life, but by the time I left the bar I was feeling all right. Not tipsy or anything. Just all right. I swung my legs up to the Plaza, and was just at the door of the Buick, when Reuben came walking up to me.

Where I knew him from, I couldn't exactly say, but I'd known him for a while. He was one of those characters who was always on the Plaza and never seemed to have any work, a saintly bum whose words of wisdom smelled of reefer and lager.

He had a scant beard and a large gap between his front teeth and his eyes were hidden behind mirror-lensed sunglasses. His long hair, which was the color of dark honey, was tied behind in a pony tail. Behind him was a short, round-faced woman who looked a little boozy. She stared straight at me, but didn't say a word.

"Hey, man."

"Hey."

He had a friendly, easy-going expression on his face like the only drudging he had ever done had been on some acid trip under the deep shade of trees and then he was telling me something about not going too quickly or bursting, just smelling the music.

"What?"

"I just saw you and I said to myself, 'That guy looks like a bubble. If he's not careful, he'll pop.'"

"Don't worry, I won't."

"This is Acacia."

I told her hello. She was about as attractive as a porcupine without a girdle, but it wasn't me who had to snuggle up to her.

"Can you spare some beer money?" he asked. "It's pretty hot today and me and Acacia just wanted to kick back with a helada."

I felt like telling him to go to hell, but instead yanked two dollars out of my wallet and handed them to him.

"God bless you," he said, taking the money and bowing slightly.

I got behind the wheel of the Buick and let it drive me home, thinking that room twelve at the Thunderbird Inn would probably be a pretty hot place to be that evening and that maybe later if I was in the mood I'd go and play a little knock-knock.

Seven

The place was all cleaned up. It was swept up nicely and tidied and the skin magazines fanned out neatly at one end of the coffee table like in the waiting room of a dentist's office and he had his map spread out on the other.

I noticed that he was wearing one of my shirts.

I didn't like that.

I didn't like that he had put on one of my shirts and I didn't like that he had taken the liberty to fiddle with my things. When someone cleaned up your house, it usually meant they planned to stay—at least there had been a few women who had done it that way with me.

He was sitting on the sofa looking at the map when I walked in.

"I cleaned up," he said.

"Yeah."

"Off work already?"

"Yeah."

There was an eagerness in his voice that made me nervous. He looked at me and I turned away.

"You been drinking?"

"What makes you say that?"

I fished out a butt and lit it and told him I was going to take a nap. I went into my bedroom and saw that he had made the bed. The bedroom window was open and I could hear a bird singing outside.

I was about to get angry and then thought, to hell with it.

Lying down fully dressed on the bed, I kicked off my shoes and closed my eyes. I kept seeing the lady I had met at the bar. Romaine. I kept seeing her and started wondering what she would look like naked and kept asking myself why I hadn't told her I would drop by later. Room twelve at the Thunderbird Inn. I was drifting around among big white balloons trying my best to touch them without popping any and I realized that it wasn't *me* who was the bubble but that I loved to *be* with bubbles and then I was frolicking between the lush red paths of her lips. The only way I could ever know, really know a woman, was by spending time with her in bed, so I tried to know as many as I could, in a strictly biblical sense. They were crossing and uncrossing themselves, teasing me.

"You need to make more friends."

"I HAVE FRIENDS!"

You see, when he was an embryo, he was thinking about when he could meet you. They came and took the body away and she sprayed everything down with a hose and was on her knees scrubbing away with soapy water. I want to touch her calves. You're an employee, you can't do that always looking up the ladies' skirts can't have that it just isn't done. If I could just make her feel my emotions, feel them deep within, hunting the bear in its cave, making it growl.

"You gonna kill that bear with your sword?"

"What?"

"You gonna kill that bear with your sword?"

"Yeah."

"You push that sword into the soft fur, but then it gets tough or you could wound the bear by pushing it through its skull. She was hiding herself in a hollow tree so you rub around some molasses. It rushes out and you're armed with only a sword, so you gonna kill that bear?"

"Yeah."

"Dinner's ready."

"What?"

"Dinner. It's ready. You've been asleep for hours."

"Okay," I mumbled and heaved myself off the bed.

I scratched myself a few times and stumbled into the other room and sat down.

He put a plate in front of me that had a steak, a potato and some steamed broccoli on it. There was a bottle of Chateau de Montcalm on the table and he poured some in my glass, then in his. I didn't have wine glasses, so we used highball glasses. I hadn't eaten anything all day. I was hungry and didn't fool around. It was the best food I had had in a long time. The meat was just like butter.

"You sure can cook."

"Another thing I didn't learn from you."

I didn't say anything and just shoveled the chow into my mouth.

"A woman came by looking for you," he said.

"Yvonne."

"I guess she wondered what I was doing here."

"Yeah?"

"I told her we were related and that you were taking a nap and she left."

"Okay."

"She's your girlfriend?"

"I think that would be making the relationship sound more serious than it is. Sometimes I, um, need a woman, and she has all the parts to qualify as such."

There was a significant pause while we stuffed our faces.

"So, you got off work early today," he said.

"That's right. I got off early and won't be going back."

"You quit?"

"In a manner of speaking."

"You were fired."

"We came to a mutual understanding that my abilities were too great for the company. George, my boss, just can't seem to run a business. He really didn't want to let me go—he would have gone into debt to keep me there—but I could see the job was a dead end. So, we discussed things and, well, agreed that there are just too many opportunities out there, good opportunities, for me to be tied down in low-margin employment."

He raised his eyebrows and took a drink of his wine.

"Ever had a job?" I asked.

"A job? Sure. Until quite recently I was working at Homokla Springs Ranch near King City."

"A ranch?"

"No, they just call it a ranch. It's a summer camp for rich kids. The children always smelled bad and would ask me to read to them or play with them."

"Children like to play."

"Children like to scream and pee in their pants and tell little lies is what they like to do. I thought the job would be easy, just a bunch of snacks and games, but it wasn't. I lost my position after I bit a kid."

"Bit?"

"Yeah, we were eating dinner, and this high-strung kid reached out in front of me for the salt. This was the third time he had done this. He never said, 'Pass the salt,' but instead would just reach for it. So, I bit his hand." Calvin sniffed. "Before that, I, er, did a couple years at college but couldn't figure out what I wanted to do, so quit. I might go back some day, but for now that's not a priority."

After dinner he divvied up the last of the wine between our two glasses and we retired to the living room. He sat on the sofa and I settled into one of the bean bag chairs. We sipped at our drinks and I decided it was about time for a father-son talk. I asked him what his plans were.

"I wanted to talk to you about that," he said. "I have an, um, proposition."

"Well, this place is pretty small and——"

But I guess I had misunderstood him, because he said that he didn't want to stay with me and I tried to figure out what it was that he did want, or if he was just misdirected, needed exposure to some perversions. He said he didn't want to go home, because, although he had it easy there, he felt like a heinous caged animal or some crap like that. He was complaining and flapping one of his hands around while he talked.

"It's hard to explain to you. When I was twelve all the other kids were playing baseball, but I couldn't play. They were all on little league teams, but not me. You know why? BECAUSE I NEVER LEARNED HOW! That's right—I never had a father to teach me!"

His voice was getting a certain falsetto quality to it.

"Of course I hate sports," he said, shrugging his shoulders.

"You need to get yourself a path in life. Not working at a baby ranch or anything like that, but something you can build on that'll make you feel good about yourself and give you money."

"To hell with that. Claudia's rich."

"Yeah?"

He started telling me a bunch of razzle-dazzle about how she had a painting by Georgia O'Keeffe in her living room, drove a Mercedes Benz, had pearl necklaces and diamond earrings, and maybe I was a little jealous, thinking I should have some money too, but I'd be self-made could open a weight loss shop burning up their calories because if you burned two hundred calories in an average sexual intercourse only this would be far from average tell them that I'd make them lose five pounds a week, catch every eye she had to have erotic thoughts during sex furies and yearnings.

"Look, Claudia's loaded."

"You keep saying that."

"Yes, I do. She'll pay fifty thousand dollars to have me back."

"I'm not sure I follow."

"I took off from the house. I didn't take anything with me. No clothes, nothing."

"So?"

"So, as far as she knows . . ."

"Yeah?"

"She could be made to think that I've been kidnapped."

I looked down at my glass and saw that it was empty, so heaved myself out of the beanbag chair. I asked the kid if he wanted a drink, but he was still working on his wine, so I wandered into the kitchen and fixed myself a highball.

Walking around the living room, I swaying the liquid in my glass and took an occasional sip.

"But will she get you back?"

"For a while. For long enough so the fuzz don't get involved."

"And then?"

"I'll split again. I'll go back, mope around for a week or two, maybe even a month, and then split. I'll have money, plenty of it, and it'll be my own. There are a lot of crazy places to see, and I'll see them."

"And me?"

"You can do whatever you want."

"You're not looking for a father?"

"I'm not looking for anything."

"But money."

"It isn't just about the money. It's also about my freedom. I need it. I need a chance to be me. To find out who I am. Maybe I'll go on one of those super cruise tours of Europe or do theatre in Ireland or something." He blinked and looked very sincere. "I need your help on this, Mitch."

"And if we get caught?"

"Nothing happens. You aren't kidnapping me. You're my father, and I'm an adult. If anything happens I'll tell them it was my idea—just a kind of joke. What can they do? It isn't like Claudia will press charges. I'm her whole world, so she wouldn't do anything like that."

I rattled the ice around in my glass. It didn't seem like a funny joke, but the sound of fifty grand got me thinking. That was a lot of money. For someone in my position that was a hell of a lot of money. Of course I doubt he'd even cut me in for half—but whatever he'd cut me in on would be a lot more than I had now.

"You're pretty broke," he said after a while.

"Well, there are wealthier men."

He grinned. "You should have married her."

"Look, Calvin, I don't even remember your mother. I know that's a cruel thing to say, but it's the truth."

"Well, she remembered you. I was there, so it was hard for her to forget. She talked about you some. Not much, but some. Said she never really got to know you and didn't think I should either."

"Maybe she was right."

"Maybe she was, but everyone's entitled to know their own father."

"And now that you know him?"

"You're all right. You're not as bad as I thought you'd be."

That night I lay in bed with the bottle of Pinch on one side. I kept taking short ones and trying to remember back, trying to remember Calvin's mother and I kept thinking I could see her and a face would sort of form and then break apart or dance off in another direction. And then I tried to go back to the beginning and re- member the faces of every woman I had ever slept with, Frances, Madeline, Sally, Mary—there must have been fifty Maries—Cybele, Marsha, Valerie, but after a while it got confused, blondes mixing with brunettes and women with mix-matched breast sizes forming in my mind and girdles and panties everywhere and then I started trying to remember them by their rumps and other body parts.

I could go to the payphone over at Kaune's and call room twelve at the Thunderbird Inn.

I looked at my watch. It was ten-forty-two.

Make a baby with someone you don't even know; spreading my abundance to any woman who wanted it less lonely on top than most people think a love-starved denizen a guy desperate to make new friends as fast as I could.

The key of course is to look self-assured and dress well.

I lit a cigarette and reasoned.

He didn't really look like me. I was all man and he was only about ten percent. Or maybe five. But, again, he did have the tell-tale cleft chin. And I didn't think ANYONE would claim me as a father if it wasn't true.

Face it, the kid is yours, I told myself.

I could always go to his mother, to Claudia, and con- front her about it. But I didn't have the guts. I wondered if I would recognize her if I saw her—if she would want to give me her body again. Not much chance of that. It had been over twenty years anyhow and, sure, she might have turned me on then, but that didn't mean she'd be

74

able to now. She'd probably let herself go and spent half her time getting the hair removed from her upper lip and the rest looking for fashions that flatter the larger woman and it would probably be wrong to take her money after I had already saddled her with Calvin, but it would help the kid out and maybe it was the least I could do. I sure couldn't help him out in any other way. And, truth be told, I needed a little help myself. A sort of reverse alimony, a payment for the gift of virility; it's been said that all men are naturally degenerates, let them paint themselves with a moral brush I never did if the primary purpose is reproduction it's one that's hard to escape the duty of, virgins, wives and whores slither into the hole all the women I had had in the steel bands of my arms me unbuckling my belt, a man in the wilderness.

"Do not cry."

"I'm crying from happiness."

I felt her squirming in my arms and bit into her as her tongue shot into my mouth.

"I LOVE you!"

"Oh, you poor slut!"

Her naked body was like a pile of raw pork. Mercilessly I drew my sword and stabbed at it nose to tail touching her soft inner soul. The enemy came and I smote them left and right, as their corpses piled up around me in circular swift movement. Blood sprayed up into my face so I could barely see but I continued to hew away, my rock-like chest shining brightly with the cosmic oil of my sweat beating off bisexual dancers the alpha experience different partners all the time if you enjoy what you're doing keep doing it.

Eight

The next day I told Calvin I'd do it. We had sandwiches and coffee for lunch and while eating talked over the plan.

"We make out a kidnap note that tells her where to leave the money," he said.

"And send it by mail?"

"No. Everything depends on timing. We can't risk it going astray or her not reading it. You have to hand deliver it."

"Like hell I do."

"I figured it out. This is what'll make the whole thing believable. She has a cleaning lady come on Tuesdays and Fridays. Tomorrow's Friday, and in the morning, from ten to eleven, she'll be out doing her Mensendieck."

"Her what?"

"Mensendieck. It's some sort of class women take to make them feel younger. I think Gloria Swanson used to do it. Anyhow, you go and hand it to the cleaning lady and tell her to give it to Mrs. Ralston, and that it's important. She has to get the letter without fail."

"I understand that, but I don't get why I have to be the delivery boy."

"Well, there are only two people who can do it, you and me. And obviously it wouldn't be too convincing if the person who has supposedly been kidnapped delivers the note."

"You got a point there."

"Also, when Claudia hears some rough-looking guy left the note and then reads it, she'll believe it. She'll be scared."

"What rough-looking guy?"

"You haven't shaved today and don't shave tomorrow."

"But this cleaning lady might recognize me later. It's a small enough town."

"Wear sunglasses."

"Yeah. And where do we tell her to put the money?"

"We need to find a good place. Somewhere on the road up to the Ski Basin. In a trash receptacle."

"So let's say she puts the money in the trash receptacle," I said.

"She will."

"Okay, let's say she does. What, I'm hiding behind a tree and go out and grab it when she's gone?"

"No, you won't even be there, just me. I can keep a lookout over it and make sure there are no cops in the area. I'll get the ransom. Less risk that way. If somehow you got seen taking the money there's always a chance you could get in trouble. If I do it, even, say, she did end up calling the cops and somehow I got apprehended—what could they do?"

"It seems you're doing most of the work on this thing."

"That's why I'll be getting a larger cut of the money."

"Yeah, so then how would we divide it?"

"Thirty thousand for me, twenty for you."

It didn't surprise me that he wanted more than half the money. It wouldn't have surprised me if he had offered me an even smaller cut, so I agreed.

After lunch we got in the Buick. He took his map and book—the book turned out to be some sort of hiking guide to the area. I swung by a gas station, put ten gallons in the tank and checked the oil, which was a little low. Inside I picked up a can of Quaker State motor oil, a couple of cans of Pearl beer and a deck of Benson & Hedges and put them on the counter.

"That'll be six-eighty," the cashier said.

I handed him a five and a couple ones and he gave me back two dimes.

"Twenty big ones," he said.

We turned out of town, going up towards the mountains.

The day was balmy and we kept the windows unrolled and the wind swept through the car. I handed Calvin one of the cans of beer and opened the other. He opened his and then opened the book and started studying it.

I stirred Calvin's plan around in my mind, and it really didn't seem a bad one. There wasn't much risk for me in any case. Hell, I'd hardly be doing anything for twenty kay.

The road cut through dry piñon-covered hills, with just a few houses scattered among them, and then sliced around a sharp corner and the big trees began to close in around us.

"Go slow," Calvin said.

We drove along doing twenty, me sipping at my beer and gazing at the nature around us. I couldn't say that I would have got much pleasure in jumping around in those mountains, but I certainly couldn't deny their grandeur and beauty.

In the winter people would drive to the top to ski, snort coke, and fornicate behind snow drifts or in the back seats of cars. In the summer the road was pretty empty. Probably the only people that went up there were a few nances to hold hands and admire butterflies together.

At the mile six mark there was a pull off with a big wooden sign with the words *Land of Many Uses* carved in it, a picnic table, and a trash can.

"Let's try here," he said.

I pulled over and cut the engine. We got out of the car. I went over to the trash can, lifted off the lid and looked inside. There was just a soda bottle and a couple of candy wrappers. I doubted they emptied the trash more than once every week or two, and maybe even less than that.

The place was peaceful. Mountains rose up on either side. I finished off my beer and threw the can in the trash can. I walked over to a big pine and felt the bark, wondering how old the tree was. On the other side of it the land sloped away and a stream ran down there. I took a leak and went back to the car.

"Yeah," I said, "this seems like the right spot."

"It's clearly marked. She couldn't miss it."

"So, she leaves the money in the trash can, fine. And you're hiding up here watching?"

"That's right. I'll be over there," he said, pointing across the road to a swath of tall pines. "You'll drop me off here tomorrow, right before you deliver the note. That way I can keep my eye on the spot from the moment you deliver the note until the money is here. As soon as she drops off the money and is gone, I'll get it. If anything suspicious happens, I'll see it and we'll forget the whole thing."

"But the money won't be delivered until the next day."

"Today is Thursday. You'll deliver the note tomorrow at eleven and it will tell her that she has twenty-four hours to drop off the money. So that will mean that she'll either drop it off sometime tomorrow afternoon or evening or, more likely, Saturday before noon."

"Wait, are you telling me you're planning on spending the night up here?"

"That's right. You've got a sleeping bag, so I'll use that."

I scratched the back of my neck.

He opened the book and showed me a little map inside.

"See, there's a trailhead down the road that leads from here to Tesuque. Once I get the money, I'll walk through the woods till I get to the trail, then take it. It's less than four miles to where the trail comes out near the village. That's where you'll pick me up. It couldn't take more than a couple of hours to walk there, and if the pigs are watching they'll be watching the road not some little trail."

The book said that the trail began back down the road, just before mile marker five, so we turned the car around and drove down there, pulled over on the side of the road and got out.

There was a big racy-looking rock and we walked down by it, and sure enough there was a trailhead. It didn't look much used. There were a few old beer cans and broken coke bottles at the beginning, but then it was mostly overgrown with weeds and washed away.

We walked down it for about ten minutes. There were junipers and ponderosa pines. A small stream ran along one side. There were small clearings in which grew chamisa, wildflowers and mullein.

"If I keep walking along this trail, it'll take me to Tesuque," Calvin said. "That's where you'll pick me up."

We had to decide on an exact rendezvous point, so we went back to the Buick and drove back towards town, then up Bishop's Lodge Road. It led through some dry, piñon-covered hills and then into a fertile stretch. There were fruit trees and a few horses grazed in small, lush meadows. We came to a hair-pin curve and, guided by the book, he told me to turn in on a small dirt road on the right. There wasn't much there really. There were fences and back behind them, in the distance, modest ranches could be made out and I knew that if one were to go further back there would be Indian land.

There was a small footbridge, and in front of it a wooden sign nailed to a post saying that this was the trailhead.

"This is where I'll meet you."

"At the bridge?"

"Yeah, I'll time it so I'm here at exactly three-thirty. You be here waiting."

On our way back to my place, we stopped at Albertson's. Calvin bought some Elmer's glue, a pair of scissors and a few pork chops. I got a bottle of Hiram Walker's brandy and a few lemons and decided to throw in a fifth of Jose Cortez white tequila, since I hadn't had any tequila in a while.

Once home, I fixed a couple of brandy sours and we got to work.

I got a pen and paper and Calvin dictated and I wrote. His idea was for the note to be written first longhand, so we would know exactly what it would say, and then for us to redo it with cut out letters and words.

Dear Mrs. Ralston,

Your son Calvin is in my hands. He is safe. Unless you comply with the following by noon tomorrow he will be killed. Leave me $50,000 in unmarked bills. $30,000 in $20 bills, $15,000 in $10 bills and $5,000 in $5 bills. Put the money in a large brown paper bag and leave it in the trash can at mile marker six on Ski Basin Rd. If you attempt to contact the police your son will be killed. I am watching you. If you do as I say he will be returned alive after the money is received.

Sincerely,

Mr. X

We took a bunch of my literature—copies of *Cavalier*, *Oui*, and *Sexual Encounter*—and cut out the words of the ransom note and pasted them on a sheet of paper. It looked clumsy, but was certainly legible, and had a menacing quality about it that made me smile.

"Quite a prank," I said.

"I'm glad you see the humor."

I took the original handwritten note, crumpled it up and threw it in the trash along with the cut up magazines, then took the trash bag out and tossed it in the garbage can where it would be picked up the next day.

When I went back in, I fixed myself another brandy sour.

"I hope it works," I said. "If I just had enough money to get back on my feet again, things would be different. Maybe we could go fishing or I could teach you to play pool."

Calvin was lying down on the couch with his eyes closed and his arms folded across his chest. He didn't say anything but I could tell he was wide awake and listening to me.

Nine

"It is time that I train thee in the way of the hunter," I said to my son, Ruaidhrigo.

"But it is a warrior's art that I wish to learn. Though my limbs be more dainty than thine, for battle were they meant, not to be piteously out grabbing rabbits by their hairy ears."

"Think ye then that there be difference between rabbits and bludgeon-fellows? For he who can wrestle with the cavebear can also crush the heads of many on the battlefield. There is no difference between tracking the fallow deer and thrusting a spear through the taut loins of a loathful pirate."

Ruaidhrigo's eyes shone with interest and I could see in them all the times he had lain beneath an oak tree with a blade of grass between his teeth staring up at the sky and dreaming of his father, wondering if he were miller or marauder, coachman or cutthroat, and dreaming also of subnormal sex problems for young people, dirt of the flesh.

"Teach me then, mine father, and I shall learn."

And teach him I did, first making him dispose of all his perfumes, brooches and bracelets and silk pettipants and then we tiptoed through the foliage, through the fierce forest, the tall pines groping and poking at our groins and wild pink flowers wrapping themselves around our ankles and vines hanging down and herbs letting off spicy smells, and soon came upon a boar. I leapt at it and sliced it in two with my knife and Ruaidhrigo laughed merrily. I showed him how to handle the bow, and when I let an arrow fly it flew like a bolt of lightening and pierced a lion's brain. I showed the young one how to kill and skin a baboon. Under my guidance animals died. The beaver died and died did the cunning raccoon. The fox died, the leopard died, the warthog died, the serpent died. I gallantly ripped out the heart of an elk and made the lad eat it while it was still beating.

"Eat ye the blood of the woods, and ye shall grow strong."

Some we ate and digested and others we stripped of their hides and the carcasses of others were left to be eaten by maggots and vultures. His hands were red with blood and he smiled and was happy and I looked in his eyes and could see his mother there; I could see her and the joy I had felt in her arms. I could not discern her exact aspect, but could feel the deep plunges of her passion.

I handed him the bow and arrows. "Now that ye have learned how to kill beasts and we have slain them together, on your own you must do it. A child you are no longer and must make it so I don't regret breeding thee."

He flushed with the joy, not simply of being told that he was a man, but of being given the duty of a man, of being trusted with the hunter's tool. With unsteady hands he took the bow and quiver and sprang off into the forest, the jingle of his laughter still reaching me after the sight of him was gone.

I seated myself on a mossy stone and waited, drinking from a flask of spirits and wondering who Ruaidhrigo's mother might be, whether some lady imp I had enjoyed on the forest floor, or a dainty princess whose chastity belt I had had to rip off with mighty strokes, or some pungent-groined lass from the isle of Tarnick, or one of the giantesses with boulder breasts that squirted raw milk I had bedded in my wayward youth.

I recalled the time when I had climbed over the walls of the palace in Xodikus and snuck into the apartments of the seven virgin daughters of Queen Riley. She, due to her hatred of all mankind, had kept them isolated from males their whole lives, and indeed I was the first man they had ever seen. At first they had not known what to do with me, but as soon as I showed them, they did it and did it well. I had stayed there hidden away for a few moons, reaping harvest after harvest from those untrampled fields, until the eunuchs found me and I had to cut my way out.

As I sat, black clouds moved in from the south and soon the sky was blotted and rain began to hurl itself down.

"A storm has blown in, meseems, and I, Mulvizeg, must find shelter—and I hope Ruaidhrigo has wit enough to find his own, lest his pate get bedampened!"

I strode through the trees and towards a cliff face, and there, before the mouth of a cave, saw a woman baring her bosom to the wind. Indeed she was naked, but long tawny mushroom hair covered her body beatings sinuous hiding imperative parts of her anatomy and she was wet and gleaming like a fresh fish. Her feet were unsheathed and honey-tanned and I wished to shoe her.

I approached with a smirk bending my lips.

"Thou art a beautiful personage," she said.

"And thee, evil genius," I growled, "are rather comely thyself."

"Evil genius I am not, but rather the hermitess of this mountain, who prays to none other than the god Wolverstein."

"Evil genius or hermitess I neither know nor care, but feel inclined to inform you that your presence incites in me feelings of the utmost lust."

"Wouldst thou wish to bed me then, brave hunter? To feel the rage of my passion? Are all you matador boys such domineering sexy come-ons?"

Her voice was at once jeering and pleading and my chest and hers were soon interlocked as I pressed forward into the depths of her cave, always ready for a flight of topless intent stag scene. Her tongue flitted like that of a serpent. There was a purple pounding and I saw an infinity of eroticism, of give and take, and I knew not which I wanted more, to give or take, for each seemingly could bring as much joy as the next.

"I have been continent too long!" I cried. "I cannot resist you! Your body was crafted to be mine!"

Together we squirmed on the hard earth, her screams

and sighs and pants and howls conjuring in me a strange zeal, mallets banging against the wide doors of the fortress. THE WOOD IS CRACKING. THE WOOD IS CRACKING. BRING OUT THE BATTERING RAM WITH IRON PLATED HEAD.

As we engaged in our buoyant archetypal raunch fitting like skin she dug her nails deep into my back so the blood flowed freely over my sides and then over her and in a sticky mess of blood and sweat and flux and reflux we consummated our relations.

We both lay exhausted, shivering, happy as pink pigs who had stuffed themselves with watermelon.

I hadn't reveled like that in quite a while, and hoped that, when we parted ways, I'd be able to find her again because I knew that as soon as I left her I would be once more craving her pith. It seemed to me that she had enjoyed herself as much as I, and probably would want me to come back anytime I wanted since pleasure wants pleasure.

I rose to my feet, stretched my body, and for the first time looked around the cave. The furnishings were simple, mainly consisting of rhinoceros skulls and the skulls and spines of leopards and cheetahs, but there before me were a few fresh human bones and on top of them a bloody head.

"But what bones are these?" I said.

"I know not. I saw this hollow-hearted weakling wandering through the woods ere you came. He was unable to satisfy my womanly needs and so I took him and ate him, for my god Wolverstein demands that I eat all men who are without lusty prowess."

I lifted the head.

But what fright was this?

I lifted the head and stared into its staring eyes and found that they were none other than those of my son, Ruaidhrigo!

"Aaargh!" I cried.

She looked at me with dread, tapers of crystal gold panic and sand pebble sex. Was it because I loved her?

"If it is revenge ye seek, do it not with thine sword, but with that other weapon that will make me scream much more heartily!"

I bit my lip. Poor Ruaidhrigo was no more. BUT I COULD STILL SHOW HER.

Ten

At around ten the next morning we drove up towards the mountains. The trees cast shadows across the asphalt. I drove him up to the spot and let him off with the sleeping bag and a paper bag that had a few store-bought ham sandwiches in it, a pack of cookies and a half gallon of orange juice.

He stood by the door of the car.

"You sure you're going to be okay?" I asked.

"Yeah. Just make sure you're there at the rendezvous point tomorrow at three."

"I will be. I'll go and deliver the note now. But what happens if she brings the money right away, today?"

"I doubt she will, but if she does I'll still sleep in the woods and see you tomorrow at three. It's best that we keep to the plan."

I looked at him with a little skepticism. He wasn't very strong. A bear could easily eat him.

He got his things together and ran across the road, then started climbing up the slope and was soon swallowed up by the trees.

I turned the Buick around and drove back to town.

He had given me Claudia Ralston's address and told me it would be easy to find, and it was.

It was the biggest house on Palace Avenue, in the better part of town. Originally, before the Spanish came, it had probably been where the old Indian village had lain and later prominent politicians had built their houses there and these, still later, had been bought by wealthy people from the east who had come west to discover themselves. It was the only part of town that could rightly be called green, the river running nearby and everyone using up water like they lived in Oregon or Louisiana. A big brick building surrounded by a chin-high adobe wall that seemed to go on for about a quarter of a mile.

I drove past it a couple of times before parking a few blocks away.

It was almost eleven, the time Calvin had said his mother would be away for her Mensendieck.

Before taking Calvin up to the mountains we had stopped by Woolworth's and, while he waited in the car, I had gone in and bought a pair of aviator sunglasses for a buck ninety-seven and a Hawaiian shirt.

I now took off my blue sports shirt and put on the new one, which was about as loud as a brass band, and the sunglasses. It wasn't much of a disguise, but it was something. Calvin had told me not to worry too much and so I decided I wouldn't.

I looked at myself in the rear view mirror. I hadn't shaved in two days and with the sunglasses I did look a bit like a shady character.

I got out of the car and walked over. I opened the gate and went up the flagstone pathway that wove through a giant, well-trimmed lawn that was the color of limes. In the middle of it, an immense pine tree grew. It was the swankiest place I had ever seen.

I leaned on the doorbell and a dumpy, thin-lipped cleaning lady who must have been in her fifties answered. She looked at me with hostility.

"I got something for Mrs. Ralston," I said.

"She's not here."

A cat came and started rubbing itself against her leg. It was braver than me. She pushed it away and looked down suspiciously at the envelope I was holding.

"Just give it to her, will you?" I said, thrusting it into her hands. "It's important."

She started to say something but I didn't stay to listen. I turned and walked away as fast as I could without actually running. When I had got to the street and closed the gate behind me I started to jog away. I felt my belly bounce up and down and was soon sweating. I had to quit drinking and get into shape. When I got back to the car, I caught my breath and lit a cigarette.

"Well, it's done," I told myself.

I felt both nervous and relieved. There was nothing I could do now but wait.

After tossing aside the sunglasses and changing back into my sports shirt, I went to Blake's and got myself a cheeseburger and a chocolate shake. After lunching, I drove around aimlessly for about fifteen minutes and then found myself at the Art Cinema X.

I saw that they were showing a matinee of a film called *Pleasures of the Single Man* and figured there were worse ways to kill an hour or two. I got a ticket and a pack of Raisinettes and found myself a front row seat.

There wasn't much to the plot and no one would have won an Oscar for their acting, but it kept me engaged.

After the show I felt like going home less than ever. There was a bar next door to the cinema called Jimmy's and though I'd seen it plenty of times had never gone in. I was thirsty as hell so went in and ordered a glass of foam.

"Hot day," I told the bartender, a heavy-set man with a bushy moustache and dull eyes, who I assumed to be Jimmy, though I could have been wrong.

"Yeah," he said.

"Business slow?" I asked.

"Yup."

Just my luck, I felt like bulling and ended up in an empty bar with a mute bartender. When I was about half-way through my beer, a couple of corn-fed types came in and seated themselves a little up-bar from me. I thought about muscling in on their conversation, but the only thing they seemed to be able to talk about was impeachment inquiries and the president's virginal purity.

I felt a strange excitement in me and needed to express myself. But guys—guys—men—FELLAS! What the hell did I need with their company, since they couldn't really entertain me? I didn't feel like being alone. I kept thinking about what I had seen in the film. Those smiling girls and everyone plunged in the joys of love. I would have almost gone to Yvonne's, but I knew she would still be at work. Then I remembered Romaine. I remembered how her breasts filled out her pink calico top and her blue, inviting eyes.

I went to the payphone, which was at the back of the place, by the head, looked up the number of the Thunderbird Inn and put a dime in. When the receptionist answered, I asked for room twelve and they patched me through. The phone rang five or six times, but nobody answered.

Go where the soil is fertile. Unbuttoning her blouse. I felt like some female companionship. I figured I'd keep trying Romaine, and if I couldn't get her, would stop over at Yvonne's when she got off work.

I went back to the bar and ordered another beer. The two guys at the end of the bar split and a couple more people walked in. My mind kept shifting back to the film. Hands touching here and there and up and down and hair flying everywhere. They felt big and my mouth started feeling like it was getting bigger too.

I finished the beer, went back to the payphone and called again. The line to her room was ringing and I was about to hang up when a sort of husky, sexy voice came on.

"Hello."

"Is this Romaine?"

"Yeah, who's this?"

"Mitch. Mitch Mazzola. We met at Horacio's—at the bar the other day. You probably don't remember me."

"Sure I remember you," she said after a pause. "I've been thinking about you."

"You have?"

"Well, it's not like I tell every man I meet my room number. I was with my sister all day listening to her kid scream his head off. I came back to my room twenty minutes ago. I'm bored as hell."

I asked her if she wanted to get some supper and she said she did and that I should come by in an hour and a half.

I went home, shaved and showered and, after toweling myself off, put some Vitalis tonic in my hair and combed it and then rubbed some anti-perspirant around in my underarms. I put on a permanently pressed shirt, a beige sports jacket and contrasting brown Brookford slacks, tied a silk tie with a handsome red and green stripe arrangement around my neck and looked at myself in the mirror. I looked good, real good.

I put on a pair of Benchwood Classic Moe Toes that I had set aside for special occasions, set fire to a cigarette, had a few short ones, then brushed my teeth and went to get her.

The motel she was staying at wasn't the worst in town, but it certainly wasn't the best. I had been there a few times and had always enjoyed myself, and hoped I would on this occasion as well.

There was a pretty new-looking white four-door Ford Maverick parked in front of her room with Arizona plates which I assumed was hers. As I was walking up to her room I noticed that the passenger-side window had been busted out. There was no glass around though, so I figured it must have happened somewhere else.

Romaine was dressed in a hip-hugging skirt and a salmon-pink Rayon blouse and black, backless boudoir shoes. Her breasts looked like they wanted to get out of where they were. I glanced at them and she smiled.

"I like your tie," she said.

"Thanks."

I pointed to the car.

"If that's yours, it looks like someone busted your window."

She frowned. "Yeah, I was shopping today and someone broke it. The only thing inside was a Polaroid, so
that's all they took."

"Well, I'm driving," I said, "but you better get it fixed
in case it rains."

I was hungry and Romaine said she felt like some
Chinese. There was one Chinese joint in town called the
Golden Bamboo, so that's where we went. We walked
between the two gold-painted lions and through the big
red door. We were put at a table near a pot full of plastic
bamboo and the waiter penciled down our order for a
pu-pu platter and a few mai tais to be followed by sweet
and sour pork and egg foo young.

The mai tai tasted wonderful and I reached across the
table and held her hand.

"You sure are romantic," she said.

"Actually, I'm not."

"Well, you sure do act like it."

"Around you."

She squeezed my hand and nibbled on her drink.

"The first time I saw you I was drawn to you," she
said earnestly. "I kept hoping you would find me. I don't
normally act like a little girl. And most men I don't like.
They see something they want but don't know how to
take it. When you called I felt like someone punched me
in the stomach. You seem like a real man to me."

By the time the food came we had already finished
our drinks, so I ordered another round. We ate like roy-
alty and talked a lot. She told me about where she lived,
in Arizona, and said she had a little two bedroom house
with a yard and that she had a cactus garden. She worked

as a waitress at some kind of coffee pot, but had been going to night school taking book-keeping courses so she could find better-paid work. She had taken ten days off to come and visit her sister.

"My sister moved here about nine years ago to be with her man, but he dumped her. Now she has to take care of their little boy alone. She doesn't get any child support. The father's a deadbeat. And her boy isn't easy to handle. He sure is a brat and she doesn't spank him enough. I think he's hyperactive."

I grinned.

"I mean, I don't *hate* kids, but I don't really like them either. Take my sister's kid. If you saw a picture of him you'd say he was the cutest thing in the world. But is all he does is whine and whine. He's either thirsty or hungry or tired or MUCH too awake. She's just spoiled him rotten."

"You never wanted children of your own?"

"Maybe. If it was my little boy I might really love him. But a woman doesn't create a kid on her own, does she?"

"I guess not."

"I *know* not."

"Still," I said, "you must get lonely sometimes."

"I sure do." She smiled. "I get real lonely. I'm not the kind of girl who was meant to be on her own. I think I was meant to make some man happy."

"I'm sure of that," I said.

She swallowed down a piece of sweet and sour pork and then asked me what I did.

"When I was younger I was a professional boxer," I said, "but now I'm in sales."

"What do you sell?"

"Lubricants."

"Is there a lot of money in, um, lubricants?"

"There sure is. I mean, just about everything needs to be lubricated. You see all those cars driving around out there? All the machines making cookies and pantyhose and automatic percolators and vinyl hand bags? All those things need to be lubricated, and someone has to sell the manufacturers the lubricants."

"Gee, you must be busy!"

I nodded my head and managed to get some egg foo young in my mouth.

When we left I tipped the waiter big, so she could see, and he bowed so low I thought he was going to hit his head on the floor.

We headed back to the Thunderbird Inn and on the way pulled through the drive-up window at the Green Onion and got a bottle of Early Times Kentucky bourbon, a bottle of ginger ale, and a bag of ice.

When we got back to her room I put the ice in the bathroom sink and fixed us a couple of highballs.

"Is it wet?" I asked.

"I don't know. It doesn't seem to be helping my thirst much."

"Would anything?"

"Something might."

She sucked down the rest of her drink and then swung her arms around me.

"For Chrissakes, take it easy!"

"That's what I'm trying to do."

She giggled a little and then let me enjoy her lips.

Her mouth tasted like booze and soy sauce, but I let myself forget about it as her tongue sought out mine and we kissed deep and long.

"Oh, honey," she said.

"Yeah?"

The next thing I knew we were on the bed, undressing each other as fast as we could. I was desperate to find her body. She said something but I couldn't understand what and saw that her chest was heaving and dug myself into her. For a moment it seemed like nothing else existed but the two of us, the two of us floating in nothingness, gasping for air that wasn't there and then we were struggling with some magnetic force and kissing madly. She reared up and I thrust my arms towards her as her breasts came hurtling at me like a couple of hotrods zooming around a track and I desperately sought out her convulsions.

"You're so virile," she said.

"You're pretty hot yourself."

The bedside lamp was on. I looked in her eyes and she blinked and smiled and then lit me a cigarette and one for herself. We each smoked about half and then made love furiously again. There was something magnificent about it, like the clashing of two great armies. A frenzy of neighing horses and flying limbs, us each understanding the needs of the other, not so much because of spoken words, but more due to the telepathy that happens when the destiny of two bodies is fulfilled.

I hope to God there was no one staying in either of the rooms next door, because if there was I doubt they got much sleep that night. I know we didn't.

Eleven

I woke up the next morning after a very few but very profound hours of sleep. I reached for my watch and looked at it and saw that it was almost nine-thirty and then I reached for my pack of Benson & Hedges, sat up and lit one. Romaine was lying there next to me, a big pile of ripe white flesh, but I had eaten my fill. I looked at her face. It was puffy but not bad looking. Technically, she was probably about a six, but in the sack she sure was dynamite and so that elevated her to an easy eight or nine.

Nine? No, in the throes of passion she was a ten and then some.

I kissed her on the cheek, got out of bed and pulled on my trousers. The bottle was still about a third full, so I poured myself a short one, swallowed it off, and was about to leave when I had an idea. There was a little four-inch pad of motel paper there and a pen and I wrote a note that said:

> *Wonderful time.*
> *Must see you more.*

I was going to just leave it like that but then thought, to hell with it, and signed it:

Love,
Mitch

The sky was overcast for the first time in about a month. I felt good. I slid back home, picking up a newspaper from a guy selling them on the street on the way.

Today was the big day and I wanted to be available for all contingencies.

I took a shower, brushed my teeth and climbed into a pair of fresh jeans and a red cotton tennis polo. Then I fixed myself a cup of Folgers instant coffee, opened the can of fruit cocktail, and sat down and scanned the paper while having my breakfast. There wasn't a word about any sort of kidnapping, and that didn't surprise me. It meant that Mrs. Ralston probably hadn't gone to the police.

Did that mean Calvin would have the money? I hoped so.

At twelve-thirty I boiled a couple of hotdogs and slugged down a few beers with them, then sat down on the sofa and started reading the funnies.

There was a knock on the door. I got up and answered it. It was Yvonne. She angled herself in. She was wearing a chambray shirt and truffle Funsters and she had a pleading look in her eyes.

"You haven't visited me or even called," she said.

"I did, but you weren't home."

"When?"

"I knocked but no one answered."

"Are you tired of me?"

I guess I was, but I didn't tell her so.

"I've had a lot on my plate," I said. "I lost my job."

"Oh, Mitch, that's too bad. Is that why I haven't seen you?"

"Yeah."

"I want to make you like me."

"I do like you."

"I want to make you like me, Mitch."

She flung herself up against me and tried to smother my mouth with her lips. I pushed her away.

"Not now, baby."

"Why not now, Mitch? I'll do whatever you want."

She had tears in her eyes. I smiled.

"Look, Yvonne, I'm just distracted. Like I said, I lost my job. And I've got this kid staying with me. He could be here anytime, and I don't want us to be caught doing anything indecent."

"I saw him when I was here before, looking for you. I don't like him. Who is he, Mitch?"

"He's an, um, relative. It's complicated. I sure wish you could stay, but you can't. I know it's rough not being able to be together right now, but I'll drop by tomorrow night and we'll take a bath together or something. You can fix me dinner."

I turned her towards the door and gently hustled her out.

When the door closed, I felt lonely. But it wasn't Yvonne that I wanted. I sure wished it had been Romaine instead. Thunder was rumbling around somewhere. I went to the kitchen. There wasn't any ginger ale left, but there was the bottle of Jose Cortez I had purchased the day before, so I poured myself a short one and drank it off and then took the bottle and glass into the living room.

Calvin would be walking back now. He'd have that money and be walking along the trail by that little stream and soon part of that money would be mine.

I looked around the room. It was June the twenty-second, which meant I only had a week to vacate the place. I'd be happy to leave.

There was a little tap tap tap on the roof that began to sing louder and louder. I went to the door, opened it and looked outside. Drops of rain were rousing the weeds and landing in the dust. There was a fine smell in the air. Then the drops started to come down savagely.

It was as if the sky had opened her loins to rejuvenate the earth. The water fell on the dirt, swirled around and mixed with it. I thought of me and Romaine in weather like this, making love right there in the mud. Sharing our primitive lust with the elements. I felt rested and ready and wished she were there with me.

But Calvin—I could see him on the trail—moving through the shrubs and trees, a big bag of twenties and tens and fives under his arm. It was still only about two and I wasn't supposed to pick him up until three. It would take me fifteen or twenty minutes to get there. Should I go early? No. It probably wouldn't be a good idea for me to be sitting around in the car if he wasn't there yet. I had better wait. Hopefully he would find shelter under a pine tree or rocky ledge or something. I poured myself a short one.

I drank it off and felt cheerful. The rain was coming down hard and in a little while I'd have money and wouldn't be living in this dump, would buy Romaine some earrings or something.

I kept thinking about her, recalling her every movement of the night before. The ecstatic look on her face, the way she batted her eyelids. So, she wasn't a society lady and maybe there were prettier women in the world. But something had happened that night, something that hadn't happened to me for a long time, or maybe ever.

I lit a cigarette.

Maybe it would be nice to have someone around for a while. I couldn't keep playing musical beds all my life. In a few years my good looks would start to fade. Hell, if I were honest with myself, they already were fading. My body wasn't what it had been and I didn't have the will power to pick up those weights too often. In her arms I could let myself go. I still had enough sexual stamina to satisfy any woman on the planet—and she was so much more than any woman.

She said she lived in Arizona. I had been there before. They had a big business in the artifacts line. Twenty grand. I could set up a little show of my own for ten and still have ten gees to live on. I'd sure as hell do better business than George. I might even poach some of his clients. I could have the run of the Southwest. Get myself a Wagoneer and go to remote villages and buy antique pots and hummingbird-feather baskets for a song and resell them to gringo collectors for good money.

Arizona. She already had a nest there and I could bring along my twigs for it. She could quit her job and do the book-keeping. I wasn't sure if she would be a good book-keeper or not, but she seemed like a pretty smart cookie—and we could be wonderful together.

A drop of water fell on my nose. I looked up and another hit me on the face.

The roof was leaking. I had been meaning to patch up the top with some tar for a long time, but hadn't got round to it.

I had some empty coffee cans under the kitchen sink and went and got one and put it under the leak and then looked around and saw that there were four or five other leaks around the house, so got some more cans and arranged them so there was one under each leak and then poured myself a long one.

For some reason the rain always made me feel like drinking. The tequila tasted good and I had to remember to buy it more often.

I sat there listening to the sound of the drops hitting the bottom of the tin cans and thinking about the money and thinking more about Romaine. When I got it I'd take her out to dinner again—not Chinese but some place classy. I'd buy her a big steak and then take her to bed and pull out all the stops.

"You're so virile!"

We'd make love three or four times a day. Anywhere and everywhere, just like gods, doing it in the rivers and meadows and under the trees.

"I'm still young enough, Mitch, I can have your babies!"

"Is that what you want?"

"You know I do!"

I didn't make them commit adultery, they did it on their own. It wasn't my fault that women's glands got all worked up whenever they saw me. Their husbands too busy rubbing their own bald heads and squinting behind glasses while they read the *Financial Times*. It was true that I was one of the few men in the world who knew how to handle a confirmed nymphomaniac, but that was a skill only acquired through hard work and almost constant practice.

The only thing I needed was the money and Romaine and she'd sew and knit and bite my chest and then I'd dress her in satin and sling-back pumps, egret-trimmed nightgowns, buy her panties made from raccoon skin or maybe some with a zipper and a mohair bra, just need enough money.

The money. It was raining hard. The cans were going crazy like some wild jazz band but then the tinny sound started to become more deep and happy, going *plopitty plop plop plop plop*. See the stars and hear the bells and taste the smooth, fresh taste. I looked over and saw one wasn't far from being full and so got up and took it to the door and threw it out.

It wasn't raining as hard now though the sky was still grumbling and I went back and sat down and the cans weren't making much noise, just slow-moving exotic dancers, maybe instead of finding another place I'd just get out of town, go on vacation, room at the Holiday Inn or go down to Mexico and have sex in a hammock, yes, I had to be honest with myself, Calvin was a spoiled kid and I'd put a chain around his leg if he ever tried to clean up again.

Where was he?

I looked at my watch. It read four.

Four. Four? FOUR!

I was already half an hour late! I jumped up and went to the Buick and got going as fast as I could. I barely stopped at the stops signs. When I got to Bishop's Lodge Road, I punched it, swerving along the wet asphalt.

The scenery flew past me. I got to a sharp curve in the road, nearly lost it, and had to slow down. The last thing I needed was to go plowing into a tree or to be picked up for speeding and driving while intoxicated.

I found the dirt road and pulled onto it. The grass and trees looked fresh and bright and then I came to the footbridge, but no one was there.

Of course not. I couldn't expect him to just wait around in the rain for me for almost an hour. I sat there in the car for a few minutes and smoked a cigarette, then turned it around and started to crawl back towards the main road. Calvin appeared, standing by a fence and waving. The only thing he was carrying was the sleeping bag in its stuff sack.

The money must be in there, I thought.

He opened the passenger door, climbed in, and threw the sleeping bag in the back seat.

"That's it?" I asked.

He didn't answer. He was wet and didn't look very happy.

I pointed the Buick back towards town.

"How did it go?" I said.

"Where were you?" he asked. His voice was angry.

"I got delayed."

"I bet."

"But the money?"

"Do I look like I got it? She didn't bring it. I sat in the trees and watched the trash receptacle. I watched it all yesterday and slept there and watched it all this morning and then watched it till twelve-thirty. No one came. Before leaving I went and emptied it and searched it, just in case I had somehow missed her, but it wasn't there—there wasn't any money there."

"Could she have put it in a different trash can?"

"We said mile marker six, right? The instructions were specific. They were clear. She didn't obey the instructions." He was upset all right. I looked at his hands and saw that he was trembling. "She didn't come. She didn't do it."

"Maybe that cleaning lady didn't give her the goddamned letter."

"Maybe not."

"Maybe she didn't believe it."

He didn't say anything and we drove back to my place without another word. When we got inside, Calvin flopped down on the sofa. He was angry, but so was I. Ultimately, he didn't have to worry about work or money—he might not have liked the way he was taken care of, but he would be taken care. My future prosperity on the other hand was pretty doubtful.

I went to the closet and got out a fresh shirt.

"Change into this," I said, tossing it at him. The one he was wearing was mine anyhow.

I walked back and forth across the room a few times.

"I need that money, Calvin."

"Go and tell her that. We had a stupid plan and it didn't work. She probably knew it was me. But I guess she doesn't care about me. She must not really love me. I shouldn't have come here. I shouldn't have bothered you."

I didn't say anything more. There was nothing more to say. There was a lot of disappointment and anger, and I suppose the disappointment was only natural, but there was no real reason for me to be angry. The whole idea had been a dopey one.

The only thing I wanted now was to see Romaine.

Twelve

I thought about picking up a bottle, but then decided against it. I didn't want her to think I was an alcoholic. She would probably have something to drink anyhow, and if not I would take her out for a cocktail and maybe a bite to eat.

I didn't call ahead but she seemed happy to see me. She looked a little tired and was wearing a sun-gold lace-trimmed camisole and melon-colored pants of twill-stitch polyester. She didn't have on any shoes.

"I don't have anything to offer you to drink."

"We can go out for one."

"Yeah, sure. I'd like that. But don't you want to kiss me first?"

I wanted to and I did. But once I started I didn't want to stop.

"Mitch, baby, I've been thinking so much about you."

"What have you been thinking?"

She pulled me over to the bed and showed me. She whispered things in my ear that I had never heard before, desperately. She told me how much she wanted and needed me. I forgot all about going out for a drink, and

I guess she did too.

When I woke up the next morning, I felt good. Better than I had in a long time. I hadn't drunk the night before. If I was with Romaine I didn't need to. She was more intoxicating than anything I could find in a bottle. I looked over at her. The top of her body was exposed. I looked at the mysterious arc of her breasts and the gentle peace of her face. While she was still asleep I went out and got coffee and a couple of donuts and when I got back we breakfasted in bed.

"I like you, Romaine," I told her.

"I like you too, Mitch."

"Yeah?"

"Yeah."

I kissed the crumbs from her lips and we made love again, gently. It was like picking eggs from a robin's nest, me trying my best not to break anything, while balancing high up, miles off the ground.

"Shall we spend the day together—in bed?" I asked.

She smiled. "Gee, Mitch, I'd like to, but I can't. I have to baby-sit for my sister. I have to take care of that brat."

"On a Sunday?"

"Yeah, she works on Sundays." She took my hand. "I wish we could spend all day together, talking and touching each other, but I can't. I'm sorry."

"But can we meet up later?"

"Yeah, sure Mitch. I'd like that."

I kissed her on the mouth, deeply, and left.

It being Sunday, the liquor stores weren't open and, due to state law, the only place where a guy could get a drink was a restaurant or bar. But I wasn't going to have a drink. It was time to put the pieces of my life back together. I could see that it was time to quit playing games and get serious, and that it would be more fun like that anyhow.

When I got home, I saw that Calvin was gone. He hadn't left a note and the sleeping bag was put away in the back of the closet. I wondered if he would come back, but didn't think so. Not anytime soon at least.

I felt a strange sense of relief. I was glad to have my place back. If I was honest with myself, I didn't like him. Probably a lot of parents didn't like their kids. And I doubted that he either liked or respected me. He was probably back with his mother now, living the life he was meant to live. He didn't need a father and I sure didn't need a son.

So the money hadn't worked out, but I was really no worse off than before. It would have been nice to have some real bread to be able to treat Romaine like the woman she was, but she didn't seem like the snooty type and would probably take me just the way I was.

Of course I wasn't so sure that I was ready to tell Romaine that I really wasn't a lubricant salesman—but maybe I would be soon enough. I was ready to work.

There was only two hundred and twenty-one bucks in my wallet and in a week's time Don would be back with his sons, so I needed to hustle. There was no time to be dallying in a bourbon bottle.

I made a pot of filtered coffee, had a cup, and then shaved and took a long shower. After toweling myself off and putting on a pair of clean underwear, I opened the front door to let in some air and light. The earth was still wet from the rain the day before and the air was pure and smelled good.

The weights were on the floor and I picked them up and did a few curls.

I went to my closet and selected a Perma press sports shirt and a pair of tan slacks.

Yeah, I was ready to work, and I sure wouldn't mind being a lubricating oil salesmen. There was a pretty big market for lubrication. I would start at the bottom and work my way up. I'd be honest and do the best job that anybody had ever seen. I would make something of myself.

I looked at my watch. It was almost eleven. I'd swing down to the Plaza, get a bite to eat and take another gander at the want ads. I couldn't put any applications in until the next day, Monday, but I could at least start to get things into focus.

There was a sense of determination in my mind. I got in the Buick and slid into town. The sky was a clear blue. It was already hot outside and I could tell it was going to get hotter, which was all right with me. Summer was meant to be hot.

I parked on West San Francisco Street, half a block down from the Plaza. Walking, I smoked half a cigarette, flicked the other half away and then went into the Plaza Restaurant. The place was pretty full, but I found a seat towards the back.

The waitress was skinny and tired looking and seemed like she probably didn't wash up enough, but I would have bet she would have been fun for a quick tumble.

"I'll have the huevos rancheros, over easy," I told her.

"Red or green?"

"As long as you're bringing it, it could even be purple."

"I'll give you the green," she said soberly.

"You can give me whatever you want."

"And to drink?"

I almost ordered a cerveza, but didn't.

"I'll have a soda pop. A Mr. Pibb."

A minute later she brought out the soda in a red plastic cup filled with ice. I took a drink. It didn't taste as good as beer, but it was cold, which was something.

The huevos rancheros came about seven minutes later and I started to dig in. There were a couple of eggs on some corn tortillas smothered with green chile, and rice and beans and posole. I scooped some rice into my mouth and then got to work on the eggs, curling the food into my mouth and washing it down with pop. The chile wasn't too spicy, but it was good and hit the spot.

An old man who was about four feet tall and who didn't have too many teeth came walking into the restaurant selling newspapers, wandering from table to table, and I figured he had probably used to be a rodeo clown or something and ended up getting kicked in the head by a Brahma bull.

He smiled and showed his gums. I pulled out a quarter and bought a paper, feeling sorry for him.

I kept eating, looking at the paper as I chewed.

The headlines were nothing but a bunch of crap about Nixon and his aides and then on page two there was an article about how the University of California at Los Angeles marijuana researchers had discovered that pot caused a sharp drop in male sex drive. The article said that although people claimed that the drug caused heightened sexual appetite and ability, this was not true. I turned the page and there was something about how the Young Citizens for Action were trying to get merchants to remove spray paint from store shelves because children were shoplifting it and sniffing the contents, and then, on the next page, in the local news section, there was an article about a kidnapping.

There was a photo, but it didn't seem to go with the story and my first thought was that Calvin had never gone home, but then, as my eyes sucked the words off the page, I began to sicken.

> *Calvin Ralston, the 7-year-old son of Claudia Ralston, heiress to the Ralston Oil fortune and one of the wealthiest women in the state, was abducted from his day care on Friday, July 19. His mother paid a large ransom, but the boy has yet to be released.*
>
> *Ms. Priscilla Vigil, an employee of Mrs. Ralston, said that, shortly after 11 a.m. on Friday, while the latter was attending therapeutic Mensendieck classes, a man delivered the ransom note. Mrs. Ralston paid the ransom on Saturday morning, but the child was never released.*
>
> *"Whoever did this heinous act," Capt. Benito S. Gomez, chief of state police detectives said, "will be found and prosecuted to the full extent of the law. Kidnapping charges in our state bring 30 years to life."*

I looked at the photo. But it wasn't a photo of Calvin. It was someone else. A kid. A seven-year-old kid.

I felt like someone had just socked me in the brain. I tried to read through the article again, but the words just danced around in front of me and nothing made sense. There was a clatter of dishes and people talking in loud voices. Things seemed to be whirling around me and my thoughts rushed one into the next, snapping and splintering.

The waitress came by.

"Everything okay?"

She saw that I had stopped eating.

"Sure. Fine. Just not as hungry as I thought I was I guess."

I reached for my Mr. Pibb and with a trembling hand lifted the cup to my mouth and chugged it down, then slapped five bucks on the table but didn't wait for change. My chair screeched as I pushed it back and a fat lady at a booth nearby me looked over. I grabbed the paper, folded it in half and strode to the door, trying my best to look relaxed, and then was outside.

A man with a heavy moustache and lightly tinted glasses was leaning against a post near me. Most likely some undercover cop and his gaze seemed to be hard on me like he had a hang-up on guys in Perma press sports shirts. I inched away, feeling that everyone in the world was watching me.

Calm the hell down, I told myself.

There was a trash bin and I stuffed the newspaper in it, as if I was getting rid of evidence, and then started slithering away. I just had to get out of there. Any place—

but I had to get away! Sweat started jumping out of my pores. He was going to come after me and everyone was thirsty and strung out. I could almost feel the cold handcuffs and someone touched my shoulder and I almost vomited.

"Mitch!"

I turned around. It was Reuben.

"Hey, calm down, man. It's planet Earth, don't focus on the beads!"

His girlfriend, Acacia, was standing behind him, her face bland, expressionless.

He was wearing a light-blue bandana headband, a green tank-top and flare jeans that were kept up with a red and green Guatemalan belt. She had on a short-sleeve dot shirt and zip-back poplin pants.

He asked me what I was doing and I laughed anxiously and said that it was Sunday, so why should I be doing anything.

"Then come with us," he said.

Without thinking I walked with them. It felt like the world was falling apart around me like the sunrays were falling from the sky and it seemed like everyone was tilted sideways, looking at me like they wanted to screw me. He was saying something but I didn't understand what it was.

"I can't go with you," I said. "I've got other things to do."

He shook his head and kept walking and so did I.

We walked for a few blocks, came to a large stone building that was three stories tall. To one side of it was a sort of a park with several giant pine trees in it.

We went into the grassy area and all sat down cross-legged beneath one of the trees. It was hot and I could feel oil crawling down my sides. Acacia was wearing a pair of blue canvas skimmers and Reuben tire-tread sandals. His toenails looked like they hadn't been clipped in about three months.

I didn't want to be there with them, it didn't seem like my scene, but I didn't know what to do—had to fit the pieces together, strip down to a loincloth and show everyone who I was.

"He doesn't appear to be concealing anything."

"Then what do you call that!?!"

He pulled out a joint and smiled.

"Acapulco gold," he said.

He lit it, sucked in a toke and started coughing. Then he handed it to me.

"But doesn't it . . . ?"

"What?"

"You, know, the sex drive."

He laughed.

"You think this stuff lowers the sex drive? You hear that, Acacia?" he said, looking at her.

"It doesn't," she said in a flat voice.

I sucked on it and coughed. It, of course, was not the first time I had smoked marijuana, but I had never been one for drugs and as the smoke rushed from my lungs it seemed like someone had scooped out a part of my head and tossed it into a game of badminton.

I handed the joint to Acacia. Our fingers touched as she took it. I looked at her and she lowered her eyes.

"It used to be the state penitentiary," Reuben said.

"What?"

He nodded towards the building.

"It used to be the state penitentiary, but that was probably eighty or a hundred years ago."

"What is it now?"

"The federal courthouse." Smoke weaved in front of his face. "But take it easy. It's Sunday, no one's in there."

Instead of it mellowing me out, it made me feel worse. I kept seeing the face of the kid in the newspaper and seeing Calvin's face and wondering who was who and where Calvin was—because there were two Calvins, a small Calvin and a taller one. It was hot all right and I could feel the heat of the whole town closing in on me, like the heat of dogs biting and fornicating and my shirt was damp under the armpits. And I thought of all the people in all the houses around town, drinking beer and balling and killing one another. All the bras and underwear thrown around and all the empty bottles of booze and shoeboxes full of pot, and the smoke of it all enveloping me, filling my nose and lungs.

"And they were just marigolds," Reuben was saying. "He had bought them at the nursery and was driving around with them in the back of his station wagon and some cop pulled him over and tried to bust him. He started dancing around doing some sort of Javanese thing and the cop threw him on the ground and gave him a sprained shoulder, but I don't think he ever intended to smoke the marigolds."

Acacia was there. She didn't look so bad now. I could see how Reuben liked her. She didn't talk much—which was a good thing. And though she wasn't pretty—well, no she wasn't pretty—she did, um. I pointed at her canvas skimmers.

"How do those fit you?"

"What?"

"How do those fit you?"

"My shoes?"

"Yeah. It seems to me they're about half a size too big. Watch . . ."

"Let go," she said.

"Take it easy, baby."

"Leave her alone, Mitch."

"I need a friend."

"We're your friends, Mitch, but let go of her foot."

I held it tighter. I knew what I was doing. Better than anyone I knew what I was doing because I had done it too many times before not to know, they just had to leave it to the professionals and, yeah, maybe he was right. Maybe it didn't lower anything and those researchers at the University of California at Los Angeles didn't know what they were talking about because I didn't feel lowered and in fact just the opposite. I was there and she was and I needed a woman to comfort me.

"Just calm the hell down," I said.

Reuben was standing up and Acacia struggled to her feet too, pulling herself away.

"It's that *leño*," she said. "He's loaded."

"No," I said, getting to my feet too and reaching for her.

Reuben pulled back his arm. He was glowing and his eyes had a clear calmness to them, a sort of sadness, like he knew all about the world's problems but still loved me. I stopped his fist with my nose and pitched to the ground.

"You let it get too deep into you, man, into your *alma*. Just smoking some grass makes you act like you want to show *los lomos*, make me get into the violence of *la tierra*. I told you to let her alone, but a guy like you just can't cool out, can't stop being heavy about everything, trying to make *arroyos de aguas* come from *sus ojos*. You gotta lighten up."

I lay there without moving. I didn't feel like I had any need to move. If I had wanted to I was sure I could have licked Reuben easily. But I didn't want to. I felt too hurt to want to hurt anyone else. Anyone but one person. And that one person was my own son—maybe.

It was hard to say what liberation might entail.

How friendly can a guy be? A guy as glamorous as me, as sensuous and as seductive, though maybe I didn't have quite the right muscle definition and symmetry.

I sat up and looked around. Reuben and Acacia were gone. My nose hurt a little, and I wiped it with my hand and saw there was a little blood on my hand.

The rest of the joint, just a big roach, was there on the grass, by a pack of matches, where Reuben had been sitting. I struck a match and lit it, inhaling the thick, rich smoke into my lungs.

Something was staring at me from one side, but I didn't want to look, better the rippling haunches nudity contact whipping, did it daydream shock you?

So then it turns out that I'm the last fertile man in the world and have to be kept safe because the rest of mankind is going to be descended from me. So there's about a million women lined up outside my heavily-guarded compound and I've got to interact with maybe five-hundred a day. I cursed the fact that I had so much sperm. It really got me into trouble this time. I needed to breathe. They were smothering me with their bodies. Hot naked bodies, lush contours, desperate, because I was the only one who could make them real. Yes, I needed to breathe. Needed a drink. I needed a drink, but if ever there was a time to stay sober, this was it.

I struggled to my feet.

Escaping from the compound was the only way. I slinked along the sidewalk, staying as close to the buildings as possible, trying to make myself small, trying to be nobody. I needed to get a grip, to get my thoughts under control; the thirst that wouldn't quit.

I got to Horacio's, lurched through the door, and sat down.

"Looks like someone knocked you one."

"Yeah."

"Sundays are like that. More fights and stabbings and rapes happen on Sundays than any other day of the week."

"Yeah, I guess so."

He told me to go to the bathroom and wash my face, so I went in there to the stiff urine presence and looked in the mirror, seeing blood in my moustache and smeared over one cheek but my nose seemed okay. I washed away the blood with water and then took a leak.

"What you drinking, beer?" he said when I got back.

"No. Old Crow. A double."

He set me up and I inhaled the clean, fresh smell of liquor and then took a drink. It tasted good, damned good, the wild taste of hope as I felt the wheels of anxiety spinning around me, trying to grind me up, me swaying out of the way and I swallowed it down and asked for another, just as a man coming off the desert might ask for a glass of water, that first one to save his life, then quickly demand another, only the second even beginning to actually quench his thirst.

I felt the heat of the drinks webbing through me and started thinking about the kidnapping and thinking maybe the situation wasn't as bad as I had believed. For one thing, it could be a coincidence. I doubted it, but stranger things had happened. But the important thing was that there was nothing to link me to the crime. Of course I had delivered the note, so there was something—but nothing that could be proven—unless the cleaning lady were to recognize me—which she might if she saw me—but she wouldn't—unless I was arrested—unless——

I ordered another shot.

"Drinking pretty fast for this time of day, aren't you?"

"Yeah."

Right, first they would have to apprehend me then put me in front of the cleaning lady and she would have to swear that it was me she had seen only I had been wearing sunglasses and a Hawaiian shirt had been unshaven and the important thing, the really important thing, was that I DID NOT DO ANYTHING WRONG OR COMMIT ANY SORT OF CRIME!

You received compensation for rendering intimate services unto her. Isn't there a statute of limitations?

So you're in it now.

Am I?

You read the paper. A kid was kidnapped. The ransom
was given. Who do you think they'll be looking for?

If I hid in a cave or hole for seven years, but they
can just tell me that I made no reasonable effort to halt
or abate Calvin's act, but they won't even say that Calvin
became aware of any kind of excitement, it will seem
that, not only did I participate, but actually might have
schemed the whole thing.

"Keep them coming."

That was what his business was, so that's what he did
and the glass clicked against my teeth so eager not there
for him when he was growing up and it seemed like I
could almost smell the head from where I sat, or maybe I
was smelling my own skin they say even rats can become
alcoholics but that doesn't mean they can have a freer at-
titude towards the human body, like when I was with Lila
and she'd complain that I was always after other women
and I told her that our relationship should be more about
spiritual growth than sexual exclusivity.

"Do you look at cartoons of nude women?"

"No, sir, never."

"Then how about nude males or anyone else nude
that you can think of? Where did you find the pictures?
Was it you who wrote the note? How did it make you
feel? Did you do it? Do you daydream often because I
was told that some people do that and make up things
do you often wish for things you can't have how did you
find out about it do you believe in laws or are you willing
to do anything once you hear some soft music?"

I had one more drink, then pried a ten from my wallet and lay it on the bar and scooted out of the place. I

started going back to my car. The ground was weaving beneath me. I was high all right drinking too fast stacked on the Acapulco gold and then realized that I COULD NOT DRIVE.

The sidewalk kept grabbing at me and I kept slapping it back. I walked by a couple who must have come from out of town because they were dressed in leopard skin. I tried to talk to them and the woman jumped clean across the street. I heard her say something about indecency and my thoughts sort of belly-flopped around and I looked for some place to slide into but didn't see anywhere but then was gliding towards the summit wondering how much time I had before I got thrown in the dungeon.

There were people everywhere ten-gallon hats with feathers in them badger skin helmets and I closed my eyes.

AMUSE ME!

STOP!

YOU DON'T HAVE ANY MUSCLES!

QUIT SCREAMING!

I slithered into the smaller hole and felt the heat would be on me tight around me but tried to push through but then cut my side on a rock but I had drunk too much too fast in the coconut palms to keep going forward because I couldn't slither backward, so I curled around I was stumbling and knew I'd better not and right and left smoke signals everywhere some woman up and came out but they smelled the blood and came to me and I whipped about we all have lust in our hearts and some of us have it other places too. Me running away, running they were crawling all over me, sinking their little jaws into me excited by my blood by its smell and taste my blood excited them and attracted others pictured myself enjoying that until with an Indian rug around her flashing her titties I was completely covered, an overwhelming agony with the stings and pains and I crushed some I'd do what they wanted for twenty but for every ten I crushed another hundred came murderer murderer a crowd acting of the border to the cathouses and rattles without reason stirred by the thirst for blood.

I couldn't go back in my hole because it was crawling with ants between their legs. Into the scabby wet and so I would make my way along the sidewalk under the portico then down going straight trying my best just stand here and flag down motorists not to be seen or heard. I didn't want to be bitten or harassed anymore. I just wanted a warm hole to crawl into. If she would only just pat me on the hand. I had not meant to be saucy and when my voice started to change everyone would look at me funny.

GET OUT OF SIGHT!

There was a bridge and I was walking over it, clinging to the rail then realized, no, go under!

GET OUT OF SIGHT!

To go under the bridge I had to first go over, so I went over, then got under and wobbled over some rocks and wanted to roll myself into a ball. I could just stay like that forever and no one would find me. I heard cars overhead. Their vibrations came through to me like waves that spun me around in a whirlpool of nausea.

Empty Thunderbird bottles cigarette butts a dirty blanket used condoms an old needle. Down below the water was trickling along and, where the sun hit, lush weeds and water-loving plants grew.

I had to see Romaine, to put my head against her huge, soft breasts. You can't go there like this or she'll think you're drunk. I had to find Calvin. I'd wring his puny neck. When I was ten I used to stand in my bedroom with the lights out and look out the window at the neighbor's house. There was a woman who lived alone and I could see right into *her* bedroom and watch her undress. How long did that go on until one day I was walking by and she was on the porch and she was wearing shorts and invited me in for some iced tea. I was noticing how clean and well ordered her house was and then she was naked in front and told me not to be afraid and shoved a glass of iced tea into my hand and let me touch her. She pressed her mouth over mine and the tea wasn't cold anymore I could taste it and I knew this was the best thing that had ever happened to me. She said she would teach me everything she knew but then when I started going out with girls my own age she got mad. She was planning on hiring me out to her friends and keeping all the money. The best trained stud in Alamogordo could do it ten times a night but my commission was too small and I had on the choir and a devout embrace until a telephone pole fell on me and after that had an inordinate sexual desire and is all I had to do was see a woman even if it was from a mile away and I wanted her.

Mute nymphomaniacs who could only express themselves with sign language hire myself out to teach them intimate gestures. I just wanted a job, any job. Sharpening knives, selling bras door to door, servicing the handicapped—well, I sure had done that before just so I could put on my résumé that I had worked for charity.

I sat there under the bridge without moving and closed my eyes. I couldn't see the water, but could still hear it trickling along, things twisting and spinning around me, my mouth dry, thirsty, lonely. Spent more time in the backseat of cars than the front but she never asked me why I came home late because she knew, yes, dear Mother, things are going well for me, I got a raise and am drinking steadily. Most of the women I sleep with say I'm the best. You would like them, though they might scream too much for you. Some of them pay me as much as one hundred gold pieces to sleep with them and they love the taste commensurate with ability of experienced fence erectors steel cucumber homeless salesman wanted tough Neoprene soul stands up to petroleum and rough wear.

Free demonstrations?

A woman with socks and a bra and maybe a bunch of jewelry but no panties and I got up and peed into the water, then zipped up my pants and just stood there.

I wasn't sober, but was closing in on it. I had to see Romaine. She would feel awful if she thought I was standing her up. I had told her I would see her and I had to. I needed a shower though. Needed to make myself presentable. I would go back to my place and shower and brush my teeth and change my clothes.

Thirteen

I climbed out from under the bridge. People were in the distance. Someone was laughing somewhere. Walking up the street, I weaved only a little. I made my way back to the Buick, got in and started the ignition.

Driving as straight and steady as I could, I slid back towards my place. I couldn't remember if I had any booze in the house or not, but hoped that I did. I felt shaky as hell and needed a drink—even a beer—yeah, I had a few Falstaffs in the fridge.

As I approached my street, I saw a cop car pull onto it. I drove by slowly and looked over. Another cop car was there, at the end of the street, with its lights on, and the second one was pulling up. I held my breath and kept going, feeling fear take hold of me. I pictured them in my house, sniffing around in my underwear and messing with my toiletries smelling my sheets while they patted each other on the ass. I kept going.

I felt like putting my foot down on the gas hard, to get away from there as quickly as possible, but I didn't, and kept the speedometer at an even twenty-five. The last thing I needed was to be pulled over.

I was small and nervous. My hands kept moving around on the steering wheel and my eyes kept looking up at the rear-view mirror.

"I didn't do anything wrong!"

That was right. I didn't do anything wrong, so why should I be so afraid?

For a moment I almost turned around. I could go back and explain things to them, make them understand. Show them what a nice guy I was. They'd help me find Calvin. They could put me in jail for a few days until things got straightened out, I didn't care.

Then I saw myself SITTING IN PRISON WITH NO WAY TO GET OUT BEARDED TONGUES SPLASHED EVERYWHERE!

No, I couldn't turn myself in. I needed to talk to someone. I needed to talk to Romaine. She wouldn't mind my unkempt appearance. She would let me take a shower and after I was soaped up she would come in and get wet with me and we'd make love, our bodies sliding around under the warm jets of water.

I went by the Thunderbird Inn. I didn't see the white Maverick with Arizona plates, but thought I saw some movement through the window of room twelve, so I got out of the Buick and knocked. A moment later the door opened and a guy about my age was standing there without a shirt or shoes on. He had a Hamm's beer in one hand and didn't look too friendly.

"Yeah?" he asked.

"I'm looking for Romaine."

"Do I look like my name's Romaine?"

"This is her room."

"I just checked in an hour ago. If this was her room it isn't anymore."

He closed the door.

I went to the front desk and asked about her.

"Sorry, mister. She checked out this morning and that's all I know."

I nodded my head, left, and got back in my car.

This morning? But then it couldn't have been much after I had seen her. I was worried. I hoped she was okay. I needed to see her. To take her in my arms. I knew if I could just see her she would make me feel better and maybe she would understand me. If I just had the chance, another chance, I would do everything I could to make her happy, us sitting around on the hot days in her cactus garden, drinking iced tea and sharing our dreams.

"You've given up so much for me."

"I haven't given up anything, Romaine. All those other women didn't mean anything to me. Their bodies were like cold earth. I was sleeping with them, but thinking of you."

"But you didn't know me!"

"It was myself I didn't know, Romaine."

I shook a Benson & Hedges out the pack and put a match to it. Turning the key in the ignition I realized I had no place to go. I guess that was the downside of having no friends and I had to find Calvin or whoever he was or was he even my son? My brain did clumsy cartwheels.

Well, the kid, the real Calvin, was probably back with his mommy by now, so he would say that it wasn't me who did the actual kidnapping, but I had delivered the note, so I was an accomplice, so how many years would that earn me and, for all I knew, the kid wouldn't be able to say that it *wasn't* me. Maybe he had been blindfolded.

And no one had seen my son, if he was my son, but me, get rid of the hang-ups, doing it in the fields with the buffalo, I was left a tribe of one!

YOU HAVE NO FRIENDS!

"But you do, honey, you do. I just want to make you like me. My body and soul are yours, Mitch. I love you."

Yes, Yvonne. She had come by while I wasn't there. She had met Tall Calvin. She wasn't much of a witness, but she was all I had and would believe me. She was maybe the only real friend I had.

Fourteen

I parked my car a little ways away—a few streets down on a little dirt road on a hill. I doubted the cops would be watching her place, but you never knew. Then I walked over and knocked on the door.

Yvonne didn't look surprised to see me. I couldn't tell if she was happy that I was there or not, but I figured she must have been. I knew she had been wanting me pretty bad for the last few days.

"Hi, Mitch," she said.

"Hello."

I walked in. She was wearing a pair of jeans and a T-shirt and Kork-Ease sandals. She had lipstick on and her mouth looked nice. She looked clean and fresh and it felt fine to be there with her, like I had finally found a safe haven, a place where I could relax and organize my thoughts and be taken care of.

"I was waiting for you last night," she said. "I made a casserole and we were going to take a warm bubble bath together."

"That would have been wonderful, baby."

"I thought we had something between us, Mitch."

"We do," I assured her.

"Yeah?" Her eyes were pleading.

"Yeah. You're my special lady."

"Am I, Mitch? Am I really your special lady?"

"You sure are." I felt a sudden kindness for her. I needed her and she needed me. "I think you're a very attractive woman," I said.

She gave a tight-lipped smile and nodded her head. I went close to her. She was wearing some kind of perfume and smelled good, like vanilla. I kissed her on the forehead and then, lingeringly, on the mouth. She wanted to keep going, but I unhooked myself.

She sighed and asked me if I was hungry and I said that I was. She said she had already eaten, but reheated me some of the casserole from the night before and served me a beer with it.

The casserole had tuna, peas and onions in it and was delicious. I was eating, and starting to feel better, and then she told me.

"I was watching the six o'clock news, Mitch."

"Yeah?" I looked at my food and not at her.

"They said your name. They said you were being sought for questioning."

"Questioning?"

"A child was kidnapped, Mitch. A seven-year-old child."

"Yeah."

"You wouldn't do something like that, would you?"

"No. I wouldn't do anything like that. Did they show my photo?"

"No, they didn't."

I finished the food on my plate, took a slug of beer, and then looked right at her. Her eyes were big and tears were starting to form at the bottoms. She wasn't a bad kid. I decided to tell her everything. She had met Calvin. She loved me. She would understand. For once in my life, I had to be honest.

I started from the beginning, from the first night he had come over, until I had seen the cops at my place. I told her about his claim to be my son and his crazy plan and about the ransom note. Of course I didn't mention Romaine, or any other unnecessary details of the past few days, but I told her everything else and she sat there listening to me, serious, nodding her head. A tear rolled down one of her cheeks and she wiped it away with her fingertips and sniffed.

"I've been pretty stupid, Yvonne. When George let me go, I was shook up. I couldn't keep seeing you like I was some sort of kept man. I've been broke since you've known me and wanted money to take you out, buy you dinner every now and again. I figured I could take you on a trip to Florida."

"You did it so you could take me on a trip?"

"That was part of the reason, sure."

"I told you I didn't like him. If he is your son, why would he try to trick you?"

"I don't know."

"Did you treat him badly, Mitch?"

"I didn't treat him anything. He came to my door and told me this crazy story about him being my son and, like a fool, I trusted him. You'll vouch for me to the police, won't you? You can say that you met Tall Calvin and that you know it was his idea and not mine. You can say we spent the last two nights together and you're sure it wasn't my idea, that I didn't have anything to do with it. We can say that I delivered the note, but didn't even know what it said."

She was silent for a minute and then she smiled.

"Sure I will, Mitch. I'll tell them anything you want. You know I love you."

I hauled out a pack of cigarettes and lit one.

"I don't know what I would do without you, Yvonne," I said. "I know I haven't always treated you as well as I should have. But you've always been available and loving and I appreciate that. Should we go down to the station now?"

"No, we'll do it tomorrow," she said. "It's already late and I want to have you all to myself tonight."

I would have preferred going down to the station right away and getting it over with, but I didn't press the issue. I finished my beer and then we went to the bedroom and made love frantically, like we were the last people on earth. Yvonne seemed almost vicious, digging her nails into my back, biting me wherever she could.

"You bastard!" she said. "You damned bastard!"

We clung to each other rhythmically. She screamed like I was driving a knife into her chest, was eager to be loaded in a big truck, her oyster-white pleasure, starved glands cut by the edge of my sword. Her tongue thrust itself deep into my mouth. Her toes worked themselves against me. I threw my head back and saw her shadow dancing wildly on the wall. She wanted me to pull out her heart and I reached for it, greedily eating at her warmth.

There was a frantic yelping and the waters flowed and ebbed in boiling spasms.

"Jesus," I thought, "if only she'd been like this before."

I lay back, covered with sweat, exhausted, and closed my eyes. Maybe Yvonne wasn't so wearisome after all. No one else had been there for me, but she was. I reached over and closed my hand around hers. She let out a sigh of contentment. She sure was a little firecracker. Then Tall Calvin's face started shoving itself into my mind and I kept trying to take a sock at it, but couldn't because my arm wasn't long enough and it was hot out and I was laying in the sun getting hotter and hotter. I was following a trail of his droppings, which were still fresh and then I noticed footprints, made by a pair of Padrino oxfords, which led high into the mountains. I navigated perilous trails and clawed my way over rocks and he disappeared in front of me and then appeared and then disappeared again, behind the trunk of a tree or bend in the trail.

"Over here."

"Ten. Ten nine."

"Ten zero."

It was the sound of a radio. I felt around next to me, but Yvonne wasn't there. I whispered her name but she didn't answer.

Suddenly I was very awake. I opened my eyes wide and sat up.

"Baby?" I said in a low voice.

The house was dark and I was alone.

I got out of bed and naked walked out of the bedroom and into the living room. I went to the window, parted the curtain about an inch and looked outside.

A prowl car was parked in front and I could see a figure standing near it and then another figure was sort of scampering towards the door.

Yvonne. Loving Yvonne. That bitch had called them.

It felt like someone had just poured ice water over me. I shivered and sucked air into my chest to let myself know I was alive, thinking so this is what cruising got me, reviled to the point where I was turned over to the heat, and I went back to the bedroom and hustled into my pants, slipped on my shoes and grabbed my shirt and cigarettes; opened the window and slid out of it. Everything seemed very still. I heard a cricket chirping and started tip-toeing across the yard and then someone shouted, "FREEZE!"

My legs shot forward and I leaped over the fence and almost broke my leg coming down the other side. I was in another yard and then scrambled over an adobe wall and ran down into a ditch and kept running and a dog was barking. I climbed out and hugged a cottonwood tree that was there and stayed very still. I could hear a siren not far off and the dog kept going. My heart was pounding furiously and I could smell some nearby flow-ers, and thought that maybe it was honeysuckle.

I put on my shirt.

I had to get out of there and quick. Soon cops would be everywhere.

Keeping low to the ground and moving as fast as I could like some sort of ape I went forward until I came to a dirt road. I looked to my right and saw the Buick about a hundred feet away. I was there as quick as I could.

I snapped on the ignition but left the headlights off and crawled up the hill doing five miles an hour. The whooping of the siren was still going and I could hear a second one in the distance and dogs were now barking everywhere, responding to the sound with their own, probably wishing they could get in on the ancient ritual of the hunt.

At the top of the hill the road veered to the left and I let the car pick up to fifteen, knowing that if the cops came up behind me I'd be finished.

Rolling by the squat hillside adobes with decrepit Fords and Chryslers in front, a sagging coyote fence and the ragged outline of chamisa. I came to a paved road, and shot across it onto Canyon, so I was now a little ways away and I knew it was time to pick up speed. I floored it, rocketing forward, with my headlights still off. It was a hell of a dangerous way to drive, but I figured getting stuck in prison would be a pretty dangerous way to live.

I knew where I was going. To the far east edge of town. I had brought more than a few girls up that way—girls who I didn't want to take home and who sure weren't worth the price of a motel room. There was a reservoir back there where the city's water supply came from and at night no one would ever bother you.

The road turned to dirt and you could either go straight ahead, to the reservoir, or to the left, and eventually get back to town.

I pressed down on the break and the car fishtailed. I swung to the left. The road went over a small bridge and curved down. Then it climbed and turned back towards town. There was an arroyo to my right and then, almost totally hidden by piñon trees and chamisa, a drive of sorts. I pulled onto it

It was a nasty little road, rutted as hell, that really only a truck should have been going up. I heard the bottom of the Buick scrape against the dirt and rocks, but slowly edged my way up, until I was at the top—some place that looked like it had been cleared to build a house on but no house was built. The view was the blackness of the hills with a few sharp stars staring down.

I killed the engine. I wanted a smoke badly. At first I was too scared to light one, afraid someone might see the cherry, then thought, to hell with it. They would see the car before they saw the cigarette!

I set fire to a Benson & Hedges and inhaled deeply. I suddenly realized that my life was in danger. Kidnapping was a serious crime. The police were after *me*. A manhunt. I thought of Tall Calvin. He had tricked me. I didn't know exactly how he had tricked me, but he had and maybe that was evidence that he really *was* my son, because who else would get me in such a jam.

I got out of the car. I couldn't hear sirens anywhere now. There was the sawing sound of crickets. I looked up at the sky. It was clear and the stars looked like they were about six inches away from my face and I just stood there and stared and wondered why the hell if there was so much space I couldn't get anywhere.

After taking a leak, I got back in the Buick. Though I couldn't hear the cops, I felt they were out there somewhere, looking for me, and I continually expected a prowl car to come up behind me, but none did. I leaned my head back and closed my eyes. I kept hearing Yvonne's voice.

"You bastard! You damned bastard!"

She must have really loved me. If I had loved her a little in return, really loved her, I would be safe now. But I wasn't safe. I had no place to go, no one to turn to. I guess I deserved it. I guess I should have treated her better. She would have helped me get out of this mess instead of being the one who turned me in. I laughed. There was nothing funny about it, but I laughed and my laughter sounded scared and strained.

I clicked on the radio. A song by Helen Reddy was playing. I listened to it for a few seconds and then breezed through the stations seeing if I could find any news announcements, but couldn't, so I turned it back off and had Ruaidhrigo's head in a bear and arrested for selling posole within city limits so no one to call my slept with more women than any man Ruaidhrigo's head in a bear skin sack and then touched her sides with my spurs and she darted forward, galloping over the sand and through the chamisa, I must have dozed off at some point, but the first thing I thought of was that I'd need to change my clothing, could disguise myself like Prince Valiant, but he always wore a dress. They say that every item of women's clothing men wore first. Like those French kings prancing around in high heels; bikini, panty hose, put on a Playtex girdle.

My tongue tasted like dirty leather and my throat was dry and hard. I wished I had a glass of water or a beer, but didn't so I just swallowed whatever spit I could get my mouth to make.

The sky started to lighten and then I watched it turn to topaz and then the edge of the sun pushed itself above the distant timbered hills and rays of light shot up. The brightness seemed to scare away the ghosts.

I was a wanted man, but somehow, seeing the sun rise, I felt a little less crummy. Maybe I didn't have to exist in darkness, maybe there was a way I could live in the sunlight even if it was a life different from the one I had.

As long as there were women to sleep with, and there were sure plenty of willing ones in the world, and I could stay out of jail, I would be okay.

Morning rituals were performed over by a piñon tree and then I stood by the Buick, in the glow of the world. Ravens were floating around in the still air. One landed not too far away and squawked.

Looking at my watch I saw that it was five to seven. I smoked a morning cigarette, letting the smoke drift into the clean blue sky.

It was still too early to go into town. It was a lazy place, where people went to bed early and woke up late, so I got back in the car and closed my eyes and managed to doze for a while, and when I opened them it was almost nine, so I turned the key in the ignition and hoped the cops weren't still lurking around.

Fifteen

I drove towards town. An old man was messing around with a shovel out in front of his house and he waved at me and I waved back, wishing that I had a house and a shovel and could hang around and dig holes all day.

I made sure not to hit any of the main roads and, when I got within about a mile and a half or two miles of the downtown area, parked the Buick on a small dirt side street where it might be left alone for a while and got out.

It had power and still had pretty low mileage and had treated me better than most people. I looked at it sadly. It had cost me a good bit of change, to abandon it seemed crazy. But the car was too obvious. From here on out I had to be smart.

I turned and started to hoof it. I kept to the smaller streets and hoped to God I wouldn't be spotted by a cop.

It took me about forty-five minutes to walk to the De Vargas Mall, an indoor shopping center that I had frequented upon occasion to do some girl watching, get an ice-cream cone or purchase some clothing.

People were drifting around. They all seemed to be smiling and happy. They were having a good time, like their biggest care was that maybe their socks were too tight or they weren't sure what they were going to have for lunch later. Some hot little mothers with their kids. Old timers sitting on a bench and bulling. They knew nothing about the hell I was going through. That an innocent man who had never hurt anyone was there fighting for his life.

I made it to the restroom and stuck my lips under the faucet, then splashed some water on my face. I didn't want to think but thoughts were already swinging and banging around in my head.

Passing by Zales, I looked in the window at the rings, wishing I could buy one for Romaine—one of those fancy gala sets with rubies and diamonds and sapphires clustered on fourteen karat gold that would let her know she had love in her life.

I went into a shop called Rip's Western Wear. No one was in the place except the salesman, a small, moon-faced fellow who greeted me with a broad smile and asked if I needed any help.

"I'd be interested in trying on a pair of boots," I said.

"Well, you sure came to the right place! If there's one thing we got here, by God, it's boots! We got just about every famous brand there is!"

He seemed like he was ready to sell me every boot in the place. I told him I didn't want anything fancy, nothing with tooled leather or anything like that, and he had me sit in a chair and, kneeling before me, grinning up at me, had me try on three or four pairs until I found one that felt right.

I then picked out a pair of Sanforized denim jeans, a wrinkle-resistant polyester checkered shirt, a Resistol cowboy hat and a belt with a cow skull buckle. I didn't bother trying on the shirt and jeans.

Next I went over to TG&Y and bought a Clairol Born Blonde hair coloring kit that was on sale for a buck forty-nine. Some Noxzema shave cream, a Persona Double II razor that came with five blades, a toothbrush and a tube of Macleans toothpaste, a bar of Irish Spring soap, an unbreakable rubber comb, a five-inch shaving mirror, some Hanes briefs and a pair of socks.

Finally, I went over to Albertson's and got a bottle of Ancient Age Bourbon and some Slim Jims. There were some newspapers there at the check-out counter, and I grabbed one. I didn't see anything about the kidnapping in the headlines, but figured I'd scan through it later, when I had a chance.

After paying for everything, I only had one hundred fifty-nine dollars and forty-two cents left.

Once outside, I crossed the parking lot and then jogged across the street. I had three bags in one hand and the hat box in the other. There was a footbridge that led across an arroyo and I crossed that and some guys were on the other side with a rag and can of spray paint and they asked me if I had any change. I put down the hat box and fished out what I had in my pocket, forty-two cents, and gave it to them, then picked the hat box back up and kept on walking, got onto a small street and after about fifty yards put the bags and hat box down and got the bottle out from one of the bags, undid the cap and took a short one off the neck.

It tasted awfully good.

My feet moved, past dilapidated adobes, trashed-out yards, smell of tortillas, the sound of Terry Jacks' "Season in the Sun," but I didn't see pretty girls anywhere, would have to do it long-distance, I could wrap a towel around my head and practice telepathy, giving women orgasms from blocks or maybe even miles away, through the walls could almost hear the old ladies groan with pleasure and see others stripping themselves bare and trying to fling themselves out the undersized windows so they could get at me.

It was just a few blocks to the river, the same river that ran down from the reservoir near where I had spent the night, the same river I had sat near under the bridge the day before, only when I got there this time, I was further downstream.

There was one bridge, but it didn't look very welcoming, so I walked to the next, which was in front of the Our Lady of Guadalupe Church, and then climbed down off the embankment and went under that one. No one driving by or in the parking lot of the church would be able to see me, and even someone walking by would have to be looking at the exact right angle to catch sight of me, since trees growing along the river bank shielded the place. If anyone came along it would most likely be some poor slob with a bottle of Thunderbird, or a junkie looking for somewhere to shoot up, not the kind of person who would try and bring the heat down on me.

I took all my things and set them down at the water's edge. I took the five-inch mirror out of the bag, looked in it, saw the circle of a man's face, fretful mouth, eyes red and tired and scared, with crow's feet bristling off the edges. He looked neither young nor virile.

Using the water from the river, I brushed my teeth and felt a little better.

Taking out the hair-coloring, I studied the directions carefully.

I took off my shoes and socks, slipped out of my Perma press sports shirt and shimmied out of my slacks, pushed my underwear down off my hips and stepped out of them, so I was naked. The day was warm and it felt good to be like that. I stepped into the water, which was only about a foot deep, and sat down in it and washed off. I ducked my head down and splashed water over it and soaped my body with the bar of Irish Spring.

I put my rear end on the bank, reached for the bottle of bourbon and took a teensy sip, then took out the Noxzema shave cream and razor. I sprayed some shave cream onto the palm of my hand and lathered my face and then, looking in the little mirror, shaved my face and shaved off my moustache.

I wrapped the Perma press sports shirt around my neck, to protect it, opened the bottle of lightening agent and combed it into my hair. It was delicate and difficult work, getting the tint into my hair without getting it on my ears or having it run all over me, and only using that little mirror, but I was patient and careful and managed.

I sat on the sand Indian-style for about twenty minutes, taking an occasional sip of the bourbon. I thought about looking at the newspaper but decided that that could wait. If there was an article about the kidnapping, I doubted it would change anything for me anyhow. A strange butterfly or moth that was almost the size of a small bird came and landed on my knee, then got up and floated off and away.

It had freedom, the freedom that I wanted and would have too.

The second phase was a shampoo that said it would make my hair look like a sunflower.

Cautiously I lathered it into my hair and let it sit, like the instructions said I should, remembering Clarabelle Edelstein in her lacy red bra, who used to always fix me Caesar salads and whose hobbies included decoupage and needlepoint. Then I went back in the water and washed it off.

I looked in the mirror, hardly recognizing myself. The person I was seeing was different. I smiled and he smiled back at me. My hair was a shimmering golden color. The sunlight caught at it and made it sparkle. I felt like I was finally the man I was meant to be.

I put on the Hanes briefs and the socks and then took my cowboy clothes out of their bag. I slipped into the new jeans, buttoned up the checkered shirt and got into the boots. I slipped the new belt through the loops of the jeans and only then realized that they were too tight—much too tight. I really should have tried them on.

For a moment I considered changing back into my tan slacks, but decided against it since they wouldn't blend with my new image. So I folded them up along with my old Perma press sports shirt and left them there under the bridge. Some bum would come along and maybe they could use them.

I rinsed off the comb, combed my hair while looking closely in the mirror, and then put it in my back pocket. I took the Resistol cowboy hat out of its box and plopped it on my head; seemed like I could almost hear it purring and I recalled hearing someone once saying that earlobes were the sexiest part of the body.

Maybe I should have bought some chewing gum, thinking it would be a trip if I started only sleeping with women with at least a one-forty-five bowling average, then I took one of the larger paper bags and put all the toiletries in there but the Irish Spring soap, which I decided to leave behind. I added the newspaper, the bottle of bourbon and the Slim Jims and climbed out from under the bridge and onto the sidewalk.

Looking around, I realized that I was in a new world. I ambled towards downtown, feeling awkward as hell, hearing the boots clip-clopping beneath me like I was a two-legged horse. It was a hot day and I was sweating in all the wrong places.

I kept thinking someone would recognize me. That some cop would stop me and ask to see my identification. But no one did. I was a new person. I was no longer Mitch Mazzola. I don't know who I was, but I wasn't him.

Sixteen

The bus station was only a block away from the Plaza, but I didn't have to go through the Plaza to get there, and though I passed a few people as I strode down the street, I made sure not to look at anyone in the face.

There was no one outside the station, no cops or suspicious-looking characters, so I went in. The only people inside, aside from the ticket clerk, were an old couple who sat silently, staring in front of them, staring at their memories I supposed—at those griefs and joys that they carried with them in their minds.

If any police were watching the bus station, they sure weren't doing a very good job of it. But they knew I had a Buick and probably figured I had already split town.

I went to the ticket counter and looked at the schedule. There was a bus leaving for Albuquerque in an hour and one leaving for Taos in twenty minutes. I would have rather gone to Albuquerque, but didn't want to be hanging around the bus station that long, so bought a ticket to Taos.

I played a couple of games of pinball to kill the time and then, when the bus came, I gave the driver my ticket and went and sat towards the back. The old couple came on after me and the man stowed a little bag above their seats and then held his wife's hand as she sat down, helping her into her seat. I wondered how long they had been together and if they had had much fun in the sack when they first met. Hell, for all I knew they were still having fun in the sack, kissing each others wrinkles and doing it as slow as snails dipped in methadone!

There were only four or five other people on the bus and no one seemed to care about me and most of the windows were cracked open because it was hot. As we pulled out of town I snuck a drink from the bottle.

Take a few swigs to keep your nerves steady, but DO NOT GET DRUNK!

I turned and looked out over the scenery.

We rolled through the dry hills, passing odd-shaped sandstone formations, distant mountain ranges outlined against the azure sky. The wind sighed through the window. At Pojoaque I saw a cop car pulled over on the side of the road, and was glad that I had decided to take the bus. They could still search it, of course, but would they?

If I got caught and proven guilty, which didn't seem like it would be too hard of a thing to do, I'd have to serve a jail sentence—maybe a prison sentence. If I were honest with myself, even if Tall Calvin had been Small Calvin, what I had done would probably count as a crime. A kidnap note is a kidnap note is a kidnap note and the thought made sweat jump out of my skin.

I pulled out the newspaper. The article was on page two. There was still no photo, but it said my name, my full name, and my age and gave a description of me, though it said I had black hair and now I didn't and said I had a moustache and that wasn't true anymore either.

It talked about how the police had searched my house, the neighbors didn't say anything too nice about me, and said they found a seven-inch Evel Knievel with a stunt cycle that they believed to have belonged to Small Calvin as well as a handwritten note in what was believed to be the suspect's hand writing, and a number of cut-up magazines that corresponded to the letters used in the kidnap note. Authorities therefore felt with some certainty that the suspect was connected to the kidnapping.

The suspect. The suspect? That was me!

How could they have found the handwritten note and magazines? I had thrown them away. I remembered with certainty throwing them in the trash and putting the trash bag in the garbage can and the garbage men came on Friday. And a child's toys? There was no Evel Knievel with a stunt cycle in my place—I knew that. If there had been a stunt cycle I would have played with it instead of reading *Cavalier*.

I'm being framed, I said to myself.

I took a Slim Jim out of the bag and ate it savagely.

Beaten up cars and beaten up houses painted turquoise and salmon pink. A few inglorious bars and horse traders and old Catholic women with their hands in their aprons. We stopped at Española. A couple of people got off, as did the bus driver. He helped one guy get a suitcase from down below and then went into the station. I figured he probably had to take a leak. A few people started lining up to board the bus. A police cruiser pulled into the parking lot, and an overweight cop got out and hiked up his pants. Just as the driver was walking back to the bus he approached him. I could see them talking. The cop jerked his head towards the bus and the driver smiled and they said a few more words and the cop nodded and grinned and then waved goodbye. The driver got on and sat down and took the tickets of three or four people as they came aboard. He closed the door and we drove away.

None of the people sat near me and the only person I had to talk to was myself.

I fingered the bottle.

You just might make it, I told myself.

Sneaking off a drink, I looked down at my thighs stretching out the pair of jeans and I felt hot and constricted.

I would have to become a new person. I wondered if women would still pay me to make love to them. I was pretty sure they would. Most women, especially the foxy ones, were willing to dish out anything for the perfect romantic experience. No one would ask me for identification.

"Who are you, you strange, wild man, you?"

"I, madam, am no other than Percival Longrod."

"Such an apt name for one of your talents!"

I could go to Atlantic City and sell my services there. I had heard that people just thought about two things in Atlantic City, and money was only one of them. There were a lot of wealthy women there and I could carry out duties for them—beside their swimming pools, in their bathtubs and garages. And if I needed spare change I would take on the less rich clients, as long as they were pretty, and provide for them under the boardwalk for five dollars each or maybe even just two. For the rest of my life I would have to make a living by sleeping with women, because it was the only thing I could do without people needing to know who I was. The nameless man who knew all about giddy nights. Thank God I looked twenty years younger than I actually was—well, fifteen in any case.

"I'll turn on the radio and you just take off your clothes."

"That'll be fifty dollars extra."

"Let's make it a hundred."

"You'll get your money's worth."

"I plan to."

"Good?"

"You must work out an awful lot."

"No, I'm just naturally muscular."

"I love to watch you sway!"

Sure, I didn't know all the latest dance moves, but I could learn. And they wouldn't care if I was doing the jitterbug or the bunny hop, as long as they got what they wanted.

I remember someone once telling me that Casanova had slept with one hundred and twenty-two women and me realizing that, hell, I had slept with more than that. It made me feel pretty good. They would try to wrestle me down, eager to see me explode in their dream world, me the romantic lead on the naked screen of their lives.

Yes, it's too late for you to turn back now. You've already become a new person. You left nothing behind— nothing but a broken Zenith television, and, well, a top-notch Buick and a wardrobe full of articles of fine clothing. But no one loves you.

No one? There was Romaine. I realized that I didn't know her well, but I felt that if I were with her she would understand. Have biological needs for me and more. She would believe me and help me. But she was probably down south, in Arizona, and I was going north. She was probably already sitting in her cactus garden drinking iced tea and reading a copy of *Life*.

The thought made me sad.

Looking down at the river I saw big boulders that had rolled off the cliff and knew that there were others, poised and waiting, that would crush someone eventually.

I wondered if she had heard about the kidnapping yet. Was that the reason why she hadn't been at the motel? Was she scared of me? But I wouldn't hurt her or break her heart. The only person I wanted to hurt was Tall Calvin—my *son*—or whoever he was—and told myself that I just had to be calm because if I panicked it would be all over they say love is the most wonderful thing in the world but who said that? Self-respect yes you hear a lot about that but what hurt can there be in gratifying my natural cut it off again, the head body. When I found it, I would stick his head in a bear skin sack and kick him, and then cut it off again.

It was hot as hell and it didn't seem like enough air was coming through the window taking it in so took a short one. There was no evidence that anyone was pursuing me, but I suspected that someone was and lifted the canteen to my lips and arched the bottle up and poured a long one down my throat if I had disguised myself as

a woman instead of a cowboy, put on a wig and falsies,
they'd take me to an all-female prison, everyone wanting
to share a cell with me piling on top and smothering me
with their agitated body parts and they'd lasso me and
make me ride around on a big brunette and I could feel
the thoughts dancing around in my head and I tried to
steady them just don't think and then I'm up out of the
canyon and the large open view hit me in the face and
the bus was going through a field of sage, the smell of it
whipping in through the open windows and I breathed in
deep trying to clear my mind. The land was opening up
and it seemed that I could see forever. It seemed that the
future was filled with countless possibilities as we rolled
along the two-lane highway into town, past the Piggly
Wiggly and the Foodway, and pulled up at the station.

I almost considered staying on the bus, which would
continue on to Raton, but, though Raton was farther
away, it was still in-state, and I was not at all sure that
I wanted to go there, so got off and saw that the old
couple had got off just before me and they were greeted
by a thin woman with long black hair who was probably
rummaging through her forties, and I was almost tempted
to introduce myself and have them take me home with
them, I could hum along with her into bed and be their
son-in-law, but went into the station instead, took a quick
visit to the restroom and then bought some Wrigley's
chewing gum and a pack of Benson & Hedges from the
vending machines and looked at the bus schedule.

There was a bus leaving to Denver via Alamosa at
four-forty. At least that would put me out of the state.
I bought a ticket and looked at my watch. It was two
thirty-five. I had about two hours to kill.

I pulled the front of my hat down low, so that my face was partially concealed and, carrying the paper bag with the rest of my bottle and Slim Jims, walked up to the Plaza. My steps weren't quite as steady as I'd have wished. But that's what happens when you drink half a bottle of bourbon with only a few Slim Jim's in your stomach. I passed Guajardo's shop and through the window saw him haggling with a customer and wished that I could have gone in and bulled with him.

A police car slowly drove around the plaza and then slid away. I supposed they wouldn't really be looking for me too closely up here. And I didn't look much like *me* anymore.

I was hungry so went to a place called Joe's Good Eat that was off the north side of the Plaza and got a club sandwich, some fries and a Mr. Pibb.

One of my hungers had been appeased, but there was another and I wished I could have gone to Christine's and kissed that pink mouth of hers and bounced around for a while up in her room, but I did feel better, grounded, and decided to stroll around for forty-five minutes or so before going back to the station.

I smoked a cigarette and walked through the small lanes. Some of the houses had gardens and, looking over the short walls, I admired the sunflowers and other flowers and bees were buzzing around and I saw a cat relaxing in the sun that reminded me a little of Madge Kitajima who had liked to play bridge and drink Singapore slings and who used to kiss me for so long that I felt like I would suffocate.

The cat was relaxing, but I couldn't. Not yet, and maybe not ever. If I relaxed I'd get caught.

Looking at my watch, I saw that it was a quarter to four, so I turned back towards the center of town, figuring I'd slowly wind my way back to the bus station.

There were cars parked along the side of the street, and coming up alongside one of them, a white Ford Maverick, I noticed that the shotgun window was open. When I got past it, I looked at the license plate and saw that it was from Arizona.

The world suddenly seemed to have become completely still.

Backtracking to the open window I saw that it wasn't open, but had been busted out. I could see a few little bits of glass in the groove where the window had been.

I leaned against the car to steady myself. It was sitting in the sun and a mildewy smell came from inside, like maybe the upholstery had got wet.

It had to be Romaine's car.

Maybe she had come up to Taos with her sister? She was on vacation, so it would make sense. Maybe she hadn't heard the news reports, or if she had, it wasn't the reason she had left the motel.

Sweet honey.

If I could speak with her alone, I could find out. I had to see her—to talk to her. She'd be glad to see me. If she was alone we could drive somewhere and make love in the back seat of her car.

I'd wait. If she was with her sister though, I would have to be careful about approaching her. I could trust Romaine, but I couldn't trust anyone else.

I'd wait. Even if I missed my bus, I'd wait for her.

Across the street there was an old adobe building with a portico.

I crossed the street, set the paper bag with the half-full bottle of whisky, Slim Jims and toiletries down on the sidewalk, and pushed my body against one of the posts. I lit a cigarette and watched. My heart felt as if it had opened up. There was more than hope, there was a kind of joyous apprehension. All sorts of plans and ideas rushed through my mind, but I didn't try and chase them down.

It seemed like I could feel her warmth near me, the warmth of her body, of her eyes, her moist sultry voice telling me how virile I was, us grappling with each other in the heat of passion. She'd discover me and I would discover her—every inch of her—and even if I could just hold her hand—us walking through summer grasses, drinking martinis on some veranda with smiles and laughter and suggestive talk.

Then I saw her. She was walking from the direction of the Plaza and in one hand carried a brown safari bag.

She was wearing a cotton patchwork halter, high heels and I could hear her steps as she walked and her hips were rolling around in a way that made me feel weak. She opened the backdoor on the passenger's side, put the bag in and closed it.

She looked beautiful. I wanted to run over to her and grab her and smother her with kisses. I took a step forward, off the curb, and then stopped. Someone had come up beside her, a man.

She turned around and then he was bending over her, putting his mouth to hers.

I knew him. It was Calvin. I could feel my heart thumping away in my chest and everything started to look washed out. Scrambled beige and blurry brown and it felt like my face was being rubbed right off. My first impulse was to jump over and seize him, but I told myself to take it easy.

Gently I crossed the street. I felt like a ghost—it felt like my feet weren't even touching the ground. I was smiling. I don't know why the hell I was, but I was, could feel my lips stretched out towards my ears and my motions and everything around me seemed to have slowed down and become incredibly delicate.

At first they didn't even look at me, didn't even notice.

"Hello," I said.

Romaine turned. There was a dull drooping look on her face. Then excitement came into her eyes, but I couldn't tell if it was fear or longing.

"Mitch?" she said.

Calvin looked surprised as hell. He stared at me and shrunk about six inches and his face looked a little green. We all stood there for what seemed like a month.

"Pretending to be my son," I said. My voice was shaking.

"Pretending?"

He pushed his jaw out.

"Why did you do it?" I asked. "Who are you? You're not Calvin—I know that much!"

"My name's Ronnie," he said. "And I *am* your son,"

"Prove it!"

"He doesn't need to prove it," Romaine said. "I'm his mother."

She smiled and then her mouth twisted itself into a sulky frown. At first I didn't really understand what she was saying, then it hit me. It was like a mountain had fallen on my head and the wheels that moved my life seemed to be spinning out of control.

"Yeah," she said, "I was only seventeen. You probably don't even remember me. I was a goddamned virgin. I hadn't hardly even kissed a boy before. It was at the La Fonda. I was on vacation with my parents and they were up in their room. You were there at the bar of the La Fonda and saw me drinking a Shirley Temple and came and told me I had the prettiest eyes you'd ever seen. You slipped the waitress a five and got her to bring me something stronger. I had never really drunk before and you acted nice to me—real nice. Then we went to my room and you hurt me and I cried but you just wouldn't stop. I clung to you and loved you as best as I could. When you left you didn't even say goodbye."

"I don't remember," I said lamely.

"I was going to get an abortion. Thank God I didn't." Ronnie smirked.

"I brought him up by myself. A single mother. Us just living off the tips I got at the coffee pot. Then, after all those years, we came back. Not because of you, but you came into the picture, because I guess that's how destiny works. Me and Ronnie went into the La Fonda for a drink, and there you were."

"You recognized me?"

"Sure I recognized you, Mitch. I'd thought about you for so long after that night. That night you made me love my body, but after that I hated it. The day after we did it, my parents took me back to Arizona. They never knew, but when I realized I was pregnant I ran away. I went back to Santa Fe and would drink Shirley Temples in the bar of the La Fonda every night hoping I'd see you. But you never came and those Shirley Temples just didn't taste good to me anymore, Mitch. I wanted a Martini and they wouldn't serve me one and I went back to Arizona with my tail between my legs. My parents said I was no good and that's how I felt. Even after Ronnie was born I wondered if I would ever see you again. At first I kept hoping I would. I thought that I needed you. Then I decided I never wanted to see you as long as I lived. You were the only man I ever slept with!"

"Romaine!" Ronnie said.

"Well, you know what I mean."

"I'm a man."

"You're my son!"

I felt sickened, but at the same time fascinated. My mother was there and she was cleaning up the brains and blood of my father that were all over the porch and I was with the neighbor trying my best, then grooming myself and encountering the dangers of strong sexual excitement and getting fresh with girls and touching their torsos whenever I could. Telling them to take the pill or being too drunk to care if they took the pill and the countless times in the back of the car or a motel room or at a baseball diamond, behind a wall, in a barn or shed.

Suddenly Romaine was all the women. All the women I had ever slept with, enjoyed. She was Yvonne, she was Christine, she was Madge, she was Clarabelle, she was all those women whose legs I had pried apart with words and kisses and steak dinners—all the women I had ever lied to. In her anger and yearning she looked beautiful—a full-hipped angel with celestial warmth between her breasts.

She had only wanted one thing, and it was my love, and so she was a little cross because she hadn't got as much as she wanted. I couldn't really blame her. Just like all the rest of them who had told me to stay around to do it again, who had torn out their hearts and offered them to me. If it hadn't been for Ronnie and his Oedipus complex, none of this would have happened. Me and Romaine would be tucked away at the Thunderbird Inn making wild love. He had soiled her, and I felt bad about that. But she was a good woman. Maybe I could make it up to her.

Could I?

Hell, she was the person I really needed. The person who could save me, who could save me in so many ways. She had talked about destiny, and she was right. I had spent my whole life going about things ass backwards. I had been playing black so long that I hadn't thought that is all I had to do was push the chips over to red.

IT WASN'T TOO LATE!

Ronnie was grinning. He looked like a punk and I guess he was one.

An old man with a cane was walking by and stared.

There has never been a woman who could ride this hunter without exhilaration I had to have her no matter what. Ronnie was clenching his fists and I almost felt sorry for him and the lady was there and I could smell her sweetness, smell her need to be loved.

"It isn't your fault, Romaine," I said.

"But, I———"

"No!" I insisted. "You don't need to give up your life for him. It isn't too late to be happy. He's a grown man. His mistakes are his own. I made mistakes and maybe you did too, but a person can't keep beating themselves up over the past. We don't need to be responsible for him. We can still be happy together!"

"She's happy with me, Mitch," Ronnie said.

Romaine was shaking her head. Tears were rolling down her cheeks.

"No, Ronnie, I'm not. It's Mitch I love, Mitch who I've always loved. He was the first and only."

"Don't say that!"

"I can't do it anymore, Ronnie. I can't. Me and Mitch—me and your father spent time together and felt like adults. He made me feel like a woman, Ronnie. It was wrong being with you. I know that and so do you. I've been a bad mother, a really bad mother. I'm sorry about that. But now it's time for you to grow up."

"I grew up a long time ago," he told her. His voice was a little unsteady. "You never letting me have my own room didn't keep me a baby, but made me a man. You wanted me to be emotionally dependent on you, but now that you don't need me, you're just ditching me. For the man that hurt you, for the man who hurt both of us. It seems a little late to try and wean me now."

"Don't say those awful things!"

"Well, that money—you can't keep it all!"

He reached for the handle of the back seat door and was opening it.

"You think to drinketh my cream?" I said, grabbing him. "Ye wayward boy, I shall now slug thee."

I slapped his face and then backhanded him and he let out a sound like a cat being stepped on.

"Don't hit him, Mitch!" Romaine said. "Don't hit him!"

I knew she didn't like it, but I had to show him that he had been bad to both me and her. My right sprang out and hit him on the cheek and then I drove my left into his ribs. He crumpled on the sidewalk. I looked at Romaine. She had one hand covering her mouth.

"Let's go," I told her.

She nodded her head. Her cheeks were wet but she wasn't crying anymore.

"I'm sorry," she said looking at Ronnie. "I really am."

She stepped around the front of the car and got in the driver's seat and I got in the passenger's side, settling down in the bucket seat. She started the engine. Ronnie was on his feet now.

"Give it to me," he said.

The car started to move forward and Ronnie lunged at the door.

"Step on it, Romaine," I said.

She did and the tires let out a little squeal as the car jumped forward. Ronnie hit the trunk with his hand or fist as we pulled away. I could see him in the passenger side mirror, a lonesome, frustrated figure in the road.

She asked me where the Buick was and I told her I didn't have it, that I had left it in Santa Fe and had taken a bus to Taos.

She took a few turns, drove through the Plaza, hit the main road and took a left.

"Is this the right direction?" I asked.

"I don't know," she said. "Let's just drive for a while."

"Where were you headed?"

"We were going to go to Denver. I've heard it's a pretty wild place."

"Any place can be—if you're with the right person."

"I am now," she said.

It was almost four-forty. My bus would be leaving soon and I would miss it and I was glad. It was the middle of summer and the days were long. The sky was a brilliant blue. We passed some fields in which paint horses were grazing. They were beautiful animals and I thought that Romaine and I weren't so different from them. All we wanted was a little pasture to graze in and rub our necks together. Nothing else seemed important now, not Ronnie or money or how I'd make a living.

I realized that I had forgotten the paper bag with the half-bottle of bourbon and other things back there on the sidewalk, but that didn't matter either.

I had never felt so good in my entire life, because it seemed that until then I hadn't lived—hadn't really lived. But now it was time to begin. I would take whatever consequences I had to, and we'd be happy together—Romaine and I.

I took the cowboy hat off and placed it on the back seat, next to the brown safari bag.

Air was coming in through the window but she was only doing about thirty and the whole world was green and alive and behind the pastures were the high peaks around which eagles soared, spreading their wings and dancing in the sky.

Romaine was looking at me. She had a cute smirk on her face.

"You don't look too bad as a blond," she said.

"Neither do you," I said.

"I was thinking about you so much. I thought I would never see you again, never again be able to feel your arms around me. To be able to give you my body."

"I want it."

"Yes, we need to be alone together."

"That's all I want."

"I'm glad. I want you to only want me. I want to be everything to you."

"You know we're going to have to go to the police and explain things to them. Explain how it was all Calvin—I mean Ronnie's fault. They may want me to spend a night or two in jail, but then once things are clear . . ."

"Sure, Mitch. Whatever you say."

She reached over and put her hand on my thigh and then I picked it up and held it.

I asked her if she wanted a cigarette and she did. I fished the pack of Benson & Hedges out of my shirt pocket and lit one for her and one for me.

She took a few drags and then, with the hand that held the cigarette, motioned towards the back of the car, towards the trunk.

"But we still have to get rid of the body."

A PARTIAL LIST OF SNUGGLY BOOKS

LÉON BLOY *The Tarantulas' Parlor and Other Unkind Tales*

FÉLICIEN CHAMPSAUR *The Latin Orgy*

BRENDAN CONNELL *Jottings from a Far Away Place*

QUENTIN S. CRISP *Blue on Blue*

QUENTIN S. CRISP *September*

LADY DILKE *The Outcast Spirit and Other Stories*

BERIT ELLINGSEN *Vessel and Solsvart*

RHYS HUGHES *Cloud Farming in Wales*

JUSTIN ISIS *Divorce Procedures for the Hairdressers of a Metallic and Inconstant Goddess*

VICTOR JOLY *The Unknown Collaborator and Other Legendary Tales*

BERNARD LAZARE *The Mirror of Legends*

JEAN LORRAIN *Masks in the Tapestry*

JEAN LORRAIN *Nightmares of an Ether-Drinker*

JEAN LORRAIN *The Soul-Drinker and Other Decadent Fantasies*

CATULLE MENDÈS *Bluebirds*

LUIS DE MIRANDA *Who Killed the Poet?*

DAMIAN MURPHY *Daughters of Apostasy*

KRISTINE ONG MUSLIM *Butterfly Dream*

YARROW PAISLEY *Mendicant City*

DAVID RIX *A Suite in Four Windows*

FREDERICK ROLFE *An Ossuary of the North Lagoon and Other Stories*

JASON ROLFE *An Archive of Human Nonsense*

TOADHOUSE *Gone Fishing with Samy Rosenstock*

TOADHOUSE *Living and Dying in a Mind Field*

www.ingramcontent.com/pod-product-compliance
Lightning Source LLC
Chambersburg PA
CBHW032029180726
48284CB00008B/2533